THE UNWRITTEN STORY

*A fictional story intended to deliver
a non-fictional message*

Peter G. MacFarlane

iUniverse, Inc.
New York   Bloomington

iUniverse books may be ordered through booksellers or by contacting:

*iUniverse
1663 Liberty Drive
Bloomington, IN 47403
www.iuniverse.com
1-800-Authors (1-800-288-4677)*

*Because of the dynamic nature of the Internet, any Web addresses or
links contained in this book may have changed since publication and
may no longer be valid. The views expressed in this work are solely those
of the author and do not necessarily reflect the views of the publisher,
and the publisher hereby disclaims any responsibility for them.*

*ISBN: 978-1-4401-4325-0 (sc)
ISBN: 978-1-4401-4326-7 (ebook)*

Printed in the United States of America

iUniverse rev. date: 10/13/2009

A story designed and created especially for you.
Bearing a message for your people too,
So hear it now, and hear it well
And open up that inner shell.
It is something that has no set price,
And determined not by the roll of a dice
Instead, it was predestined and preconceived
As to save you from that which you would have grieved
It gently speaks to your heart and to your soul
And reveals yourself, as a whole
Not confined, nor restricted
But free, and emancipated
Composed by a collective hand
In what only seems to be a distant land
Offered to you now is my assurances of God's love,
And a request that your mind be opened, like the wings of a dove.

What is this strange world in which we live our day to day lives? When did it begin and where will it ever end? Who is responsible for its creation and how did they do it? Why have we always asked these important questions, but have never been truly satisfied with the answers that we have received? The period of time that I have experienced on the planet Earth was very interesting indeed! I found myself amidst the dawning of eternity and during the dusk of time, except there was no nightfall to intervene. Like a dual twilight zone, but of galactic proportions.

Truly, it was a pivotal point in history for humankind and all beings alike. A global spiritual shift that can be accredited to a simple knowledge or wisdom that suddenly became apparent within our collective vision. I have only witnessed a relatively small fraction of this unprecedented awakening, yet this wisdom had been presented very clearly before me. It cannot be easily explained using mere words or symbols, because it really goes beyond all forms. It was not born out of our distorted values and conflicting thoughts.

Instead, it is an eternal existence of love and pure sense of being that forever abide within us. The veil is now being lifted right before our eyes and revealing to us what has always been. What we had thought of as sins worthy of condemning us to hell turned out to be completely meaningless. What we thought was reality, turned out to be a dream. What we valued turned to dust and what we could never trust, stood strong. The walls came down!

Hi! My name is Mike Love, or at least that was my name. My body is deceased now, so I no longer go by this name. In fact I don't have any name, or anything else that I had while I was a body. All of these things ceased to be, but I did not. I am still here in this place where I always was, forever dwelling behind these eyes, but now without a physical means of communication. No mouth to speak, nor a hand to write.

This is the ironic part of life and the very reason that this story must be told. One will await their impending death and only when it occurs do they find it to be untrue. I was told this information during my physical life, but unfortunately did not actually believe it until now. If only I had understood this concept earlier, it would have relieved a lot of needless heartache. I really believed that I was dying, and to be honest, it was the most fearful thought that I'd ever had.

I died in the hospital, holding the hand of my beloved wife Sharon, as she cried. I had been inflicted with cancer and somehow this relentless disease was able to completely destroy my body in less than six months. It was a very painful time in my life, not so much physically, but emotionally. I felt horrible for putting Sharon through it, and I would give anything if only I could go back, and tell her this story.

As I took my final gasping breath on that hospital bed I was expecting to simply cease to exist, but of course that's not what happened at all. I felt my last exhale proceeded by my final heartbeat and then something completely unexpected happened. I lifted up out of my body and felt free of it. I was up above everyone else in the room and had no body to confine me.

No breath, nor a heartbeat, but there I was. Watching as the nurses pulled a sheet over my body's face and my wife Sharon burst into a rage of tears. There was nothing that I could do to comfort her and this was a terrible feeling indeed! So for the next three hours, Sharon and I cried alone in that room, but she didn't know that I was there. She was crying because I was no longer with her, and I was crying because I could not tell her that I was. It was tragic to say the least.

Suddenly, the door opened up, and one of the nurses said something to my wife. Then they both left the room and I was left there all alone. "What now?" I thought, as I looked around the lifeless room. There was only the presence of my dead body and me who was floating above it. What I would do to take it all back, what I would do to make things right again. I should not have squandered the delicate time that I had, but should have used it precariously, to spread the truth.

Just as I had this thought of remorse, the room disappeared before my eyes and something occurred that I did not expect. I was offered and I immediately accepted the strange opportunity to re-experience my life. Then it happened. I went through every little physical experience since my birth and felt the wrath of every little coinciding feeling. It seemed like an instant, but somehow it encapsulated my entire lifetime. Well, most of it anyway.

I stop here at this point. I will begin seven months prior to my death and I will tell you why. It was at this same point that a series of unpredictable events led me to a lady and graciously she offered me incredible wisdom I could not deny. She understood life better than anyone I had ever met, and she held nothing back. At the time I did think that she was a little bit crazy, but of course now I can see how sane she really was.

So it is here that I have consciously decided to slow down and carefully examine this integral part of my life experience. I could allow it to slip by within an instant, but I feel that it is in dire need of review. So, this is the tale that I would tell to the world, had I a mouth to speak. This is the book that I would give to the world, had I a hand to write. This is the wisdom that I shall give to you, as it was so generously given to me.

Chapter 1

The story begins just as Sharon was leaving to visit her sister Ruth in California and, coincidentally, just as I was getting off of work for a six month period. I had been very much looking forward to spending time with my love, but now it would have to wait. Her sister needed her and Sharon is of the type who simply finds it impossible to say no. Ruth had her wrapped around her finger and Sharon would jump on a plane after a single call. I was a little disappointed that she would be leaving, but I knew that I could deal with it.

We composed a bond that could never be broken. Ever since we were teenagers, Sharon and I had been the best of friends. We just seemed to click together like two pieces of a jig-saw puzzle and fit perfectly within the whole. We were completely dependent upon each other, but this was not always a bad thing. Each of us made up for the other's weaknesses. Like Romeo and Juliet, or any other couple that were madly in love. We were meant for each other, and destined to be together forever, joined as one.

We enjoyed a pleasant life together just east of the Rocky Mountains in beautiful British Columbia. Our small bungalow was on the outskirts of Sullivan, a town of 3000. While we enjoyed the convenience of being a five minute drive from downtown, we were really country folk at heart. That is where we spent most of our free time together. Hiking, fishing, picnics by the lake; these were the activities we enjoyed most. We grabbed any chance to get outdoors and take in nature's beauty. Unfortunately, I was only home half the time. Work kept me away from home the rest of the time. While I was gone Sharon would be 'holding the fort', as I'd often say. She was an artist, and she would paint the landscape scenery of the mountains.

Sometimes I would even go with her to some of her favourite sites and just sit there for hours while she created artwork. It never ceased to amaze me how she could take a blank canvas and turn it into a carbon copy of the scene right in front of me. The purples and pinks, the glistening snow on the mountain peaks, I thought that every painting was brilliant, truly a gift from the heavens. Looking at her paintings, I was not just seeing them with my eyes. I experienced them with all five senses; they drew me right into the moment. The only problem was that no one else seemed to feel the same way, and as a result she had a lot of trouble making any money from them.

Luckily, finances were not a problem, as I made enough money for the both of us. I had a decent paying job, and I was only a labourer. The reason for the decent pay was the location and the danger that my job entailed. I worked in a diamond mine and this job took me north to the Yukon Territories. It was above the Arctic Circle where the sun only shows itself half the year. It was cold, lonely, and just an all out brutal test of one's sanity. Often times I would threaten to quit, but the money would always keep me from doing it. There was danger pay, isolation pay, and other benefits as well.

My job was our only means of income. It was enough to pay for our house and to keep us warm in the winter. I had a truck and she had a car. We didn't have very much more than that, but I suppose that was all that we needed. We had no kids and no plans to have any, which was a typical choice for people of our generation. Our lives were being lived, and I think that we both found meaning simply in that.

I gave her a ride to the airport in my old Ford truck and I recall the scene as I pulled up to the front doors very well. There were people coming in and out of the sliding glass doors at random and the frantic hustle and bustle of eager travellers was apparent. Some were in a mad rush just to get inside and others were simply trying to get out of their way. Taxis pulled up while people rushed to the curb with their suitcases in tow. Children cried, parents argued and an older couple looked completely flustered. It seemed rather ridiculous to me. It was nothing like the soothing comfort of country life, a totally different environment than to which I was accustomed.

"Alright," Sharon said as she opened the door. "Are you sure that you are going to get along fine without me?"

"No," I said jokingly. "What am I going to do without you? How am I supposed to dry the dishes without you to wash them for me first?" She laughed, and opened the door. I could see her rolling her eyes.

"You'll be fine," she said, as she was leaning over to kiss me. "I'll see you in a few weeks. I love you."

"Love you too babe," I said, as she was stepping outside. She closed the door behind her, and I watched as she walked towards the airport. Her hair and dress were blowing in the wind, but such things would never bother her. She was as stable as the ground, but she could also be as fluent as the wind. Her overall personality was unlike anyone else, and totally unique to her. She glanced back at me once before entering the building, and it was enough to make me smile. I knew that she loved me, and I loved knowing this.

I couldn't help but think about how lucky I was to have her. She was beautiful. She had long blond hair, and the most perfect slim little figure. Many times I recall having to fight off other guys, as the whole world seemed to want her. She was the perfect woman, I thought, but how did I get her? It was remarkable that I ended up being the guy to be with her. I had gone through a savage war of conflicting youthful hormones, and somehow had come out victorious. At that moment, I truly appreciated Sharon, and I thought about the good times that we had.

I recall the first night that we met, and how it was like finding the one person in the world who could understand me. It was the night of a high school dance, but the dance was over far earlier than anyone had anticipated. Apparently there had been a fight and they had to shut it down early. My friends and I were out in the parking lot getting drunk when all of this was going on. Our plan had been to get really hammered before going in. Suddenly crowds of people started pouring out of the doors and scattering throughout the parking lot.

Then Sharon walked outside and all of my friends started howling and whistling at her. I felt sorry for her, as she seemed to be offended by their behaviour. So I chased after her, abandoning my friends. They thought that I was an idiot, but I didn't care. I caught up to her and politely offered to walk her home like a gentleman. She accepted my offer, and we ended up walking twice as far as her house that night. We talked for hours on end, and divulged our deepest thoughts to one another. It was a beautiful experience, one which I will never forget.

I pulled into the driveway, and walked into our little two bedroom house. We didn't have a very large house, but it did have a garage. That was enough to make me happy. The garage was my sanctuary when I needed it, a place where I could screw around and build things from time to time. I walked through the garage into the kitchen, and set my keys down on the counter. I pulled out a chair from the table, and sat down very slowly.

As I sat down in the chair I noticed how dark and empty the house seemed to be. Without Sharon here I had no one to talk to, and she would be gone for about three weeks. It was a span of time that I was not looking forward to, and already I was beginning to miss her. I got up and grabbed a beer out of the fridge, and stood there wondering what to do. Surely this lonely period of time would be a test of my sanity. Hopefully I would find something to occupy my mind.

"Oh shit" I said to myself quietly, as I walked into the living room plumping myself on the couch. This is going to be a long three weeks, I thought, and I clicked on the TV. There was a nature show on, but it was talking about birds, and it did not appeal to my interest. Flicking through the channels I realized just how much garbage they assume people will watch. Disgusted, I flicked it off, and lay down across the couch. I lay there thinking about how much more fun it was when Sharon was there.

"What am I going to do for three weeks"? I thought. There was hardly anything to do, except to delve into the mindless world of watching TV. All the while that I was at work I had been dreaming of Sharon and preparing mental plans of beautiful times ahead. Now it all had to be put on hold, and I was left alone to entertain my own mind. The very thought of keeping myself busy was depressing, but I knew that there had to be something.

Then it hit me, I'd go camping up in the mountains. I always loved a good adventure, and that would be more than enough to keep myself busy. When I was a kid I used to dream about going camping up in the mountains and at least make an attempt at living off of the land. Every time that I tried to get my friends to go they always decided not to, and I was too young to go by myself. They would rather stay home with the luxuries of modern life.

"There is nothing that can stop me this time", I thought, and it might do me some good to be alone for a while. I had to deal with people all the time at work and it could get frustrating. If I went camping then there would be no one around to interrupt my thoughts and perhaps I would be better able to appreciate the beauty of nature. I was starting to get excited now, and I chugged the last half of my beer in celebration.

I jumped off of the couch and shouted, "Nothing can stop me now." I knew full well that there was no one around to hear me, and that was what I had always loved about living in the country. The nearest house was two kilometres away and any of the noises that I made did not fall on my neighbours' ears. I felt full of energy and had a sudden intuition that this trip was just what I needed.

I figured being in the wilderness should inspire me to further explore my theories about how life mysteriously appeared on earth, and how it evolved into the diverse world that we know today. All of my life I had been pushing the limits of the understanding of the universe, and trying to expand the limited spectrum of recorded human history. Typically it is well educated people who make these amazing discoveries and open up entire new fields of study. My one desire was to break such stereotypes and score one for the underdogs. It would be an inspiration to all of those who could not afford an education, and to those simply too proud to acquire one.

I believed that I would eventually become this inspirational figure, but I was not there yet. There was still much to be thought about, and much more to be considered. Most people still thought that my theories were crazy and to me this was very understandable since they were usually pretty farfetched ideas. Often blurring any distinctions between what was known as fact and what has always been pure myth. I tended to bring fact and myth together into one logical sequence of events and consequentially I always ended up with a whole new original story.

My latest theory is that once upon a time the moon struck the planet Mars and left a large gash in Mars' surface. This gash is now known as Valles Marineris and it is enormous in size. Of course, this all would have taken place a very long time ago and it was a time in which I believe Mars fostered life. This event would have destroyed that life and eliminated any chance of potential re-growth. The moon would have ripped away any essential nutrients of life that lingered in the air and in the water. No hope would be left for the now lifeless planet.

Now of course it was not a collision massive enough to stop the moon in its path, but rather it slowed down the moon just enough to be caught in the orbit of nearby Earth. Trailing behind the moon were the atmosphere and water from Mars. Being apart from the moon, all of this atmosphere and water would have succumbed to the gravity of the Earth. The Earth would have immediately become a foundation for growth. This could have been the event that sparked life on Earth, but at the same time it also may have destroyed life on Mars.

"It doesn't matter now", I thought, as I realized that I had been in a daze while thinking about my glorious new theory. I walked out to the garage and looked for the tent that had gone unused for way too long. Sure enough, it was at the back of one of the shelving units, covered in a thin layer of dust. Then I packed some food, blankets and the tent into the back of the truck. I decided to call Sharon. It rang five times, and then Ruth finally answered.

"Hello," she said.

"Hey Ruth, how are you and Sharon getting along?" I asked.

"Wonderful," she said. "Sharon can tell you all about it, so hold on." I could hear Ruth call her, and Sharon screaming something back at her. After a minute she came to the phone.

"Hi honey!" she said, "do you miss me already?"

"Yeah I do actually," I said. "It's weird being here without you."

"Oh, I know," she said. "I wish you could come here with me."

"Yeah, right," I said. "Ruth and I do not get along, you know that."

"Well, I wish you did," she said. "It's too bad that everyone can't get along with each other," she said.

"Maybe someday," I said. "Anyway, I've decided to go camping up in the mountains."

"What? Camping?" she exclaimed. "You're crazy!"

"I know," I said right away, and we both started to laugh.

"Well, if you go camping," she said, "I want you to be really careful and make sure you bring your phone."

"Yeah, I will, but I have to go now before it gets too dark," I said.

"Okay, I love you," she said.

"I love you too babe," I said, and then I hung up. Somehow I felt that this trip would be good for the both of us, that she would in some way benefit from it as well. As if my sanity and well being were hers too, and that the beauty I would see out there she would extract from me later. I packed up a few more things, and jumped into the truck.

It was a glorious day as I pulled out of the driveway. It had rained during the morning and the road was still wet in places. There were a few snowflakes slowly falling, but the sun was unimpeded by clouds and shining majestically. I was struck by the beauty of it all and for some reason I felt extremely happy.

"This will be a wonderful day", I thought. "Being alone isn't so bad". On the horizon the mountains loomed over the land and they seemed to glow with radiance. The wilderness was calling me; I couldn't help but answer.

It would be about a two hour drive and the sun was already two thirds of the way across the sky. I put on my favourite Bob Marley album and pressed the gas pedal down until I could feel the floor underneath. There was a good spot that I had in mind for camping, but it would be impossible to find it in the dark. I started thinking that I may have miscalculated and slightly underestimated the lapse of time between arrival and departure. It was going to be a close call. The happiness I had felt when leaving the house was now suppressed and was being taken over by fear.

After an hour and a half, I could tell that I was almost there, but there was still quite a distance to go. The road was flat and I was beginning to approach a small town that was close to the base of the mountains. I looked at the fuel gauge and knew that I had to stop soon. The truck needed fuel, and so did I. The desire for me to find a liquor store, and buy a few beers was incredible. I was never an alcoholic, but my God, I was thirsty for beer! I decided that I would search the town high and low if I had to and one way or another I was going to get drunk.

I pulled into the first gas station I saw and filled up the old Ford. Surprisingly, there was a liquor store directly across the street from the gas station. I drove across the street after filling up and ran inside. It only took me a second to find twelve of my favourite beer and I quickly walked to the checkout with the shortest line. There were two people ahead of me and they were both older than I; a woman in what I guessed was her late thirties and an old man who looked to be at least seventy years old. He had a cane in one hand, a bottle of wine in the other.

"Thank you," the woman said as she received her change and walked out of the store holding a quart of whiskey. The old man approached the counter and set down his bottle of wine. He slowly pulled out his wallet from his back pocket. I noticed that his hand was shaking.

"Oh, great", I thought, this old man is going to take forever. Very slowly he searched for the appropriate bill. It almost seemed as if he were stalling me on purpose. Now I was even more worried that I wouldn't get to the mountain soon enough. The possibility of having to turn back became much more probable.

Just then, something happened that caused the cashier to

look perplexed. He looked over at the other two cashiers, but they were looking at him with confused expressions as well.

"I think the computers are down, so I'll have to get the manager," he told the old man.

"This is a disaster", I thought. "There is no way that I'll get there on time now, and my entire plans may be ruined". The old man looked calm.

"That's okay," he said to the cashier, "everything happens for a reason". His voice was low and raspy. Then he looked at me out of the corner of his eye, and revealed a smirk that made me even more furious.

"What the hell was that?" I thought, "Everything happens for a reason! How could he make such a statement? He has no idea what I'm doing or where I'm going. He doesn't even know who I am, and yet he thinks that he can make such a claim. He has no way of judging whether or not there is a reason for this bullshit". It was infuriating just to look at the senile old man, and I could almost feel my blood pressure rising along with my impatience.

The cashier had been in the manager's office and was now returning with the manager behind him. There was also a young couple behind me now and every other line-up had increased by a few people as well. The manager was a highly overweight, middle-aged man with greying hair and the mere sight of him was almost enough to bring someone down. He had a depressing look on his face, as if to signify that his job was one that he truly despised. He walked to the front of the store and stopped right in the center to face the forming crowd.

"Attention everyone, please," his voice boomed throughout the store in a deep tone. "The computers are down at the moment, and we cannot make any more transactions until they are back up". He paused for a second, and looked around to see if everyone was listening. "We are extremely sorry for this inconvenience and we will do everything that we can to get the computers going as quickly as possible. So please be patient with us for a few moments, and we will be back in business in no time. Thank you."

With that, he swiftly walked back into his office, and slammed the door closed. The young couple behind me were giggling and making jokes about the size of the manager. I was fuming and felt like smashing my beer on the floor in disgust. I had to leave soon, but I figured that as soon as I left, the computers would work again. That was the kind of luck that I always seemed to have. Murphy's Law plagued my everyday life. The old man was standing patiently, watching as the manager and cashiers frantically tried to figure out what was wrong.

It took about twenty five minutes of my silent suffering before they finally got the computers working again. The line-ups had grown to perhaps twenty people per checkout and people were getting very restless. Of course, the old man took his sweet time fumbling around for money in his wallet, delaying me even further. Finally it was my turn and I had the exact change already in my hand. It took me only a second and I was out the door.

As I walked across the parking lot, the sun was poised just above the horizon. It threatened me with its inevitable setting. I threw the beer in the back of the truck and hopped in the front. As I started up the old girl, I noticed the old man sitting in a white Oldsmobile only a few parking spaces away. He was staring at me and he had that same infuriating smirk on his face. I stared back at him for only a second, making sure to give him the evil eye. Then I laid a strip of rubber as I left, just for spite.

"Everything happens for a reason", I thought again. "Yeah, right, what do you know old man?" I looked in the rear view mirror and could see him still staring at the spot where I had been parked. His face now revealed a huge grin and he seemed to be almost laughing to himself. I couldn't even begin to imagine what that strange old man was thinking about, but I sure was glad to get out of there.

As soon as I got out of town, I pinned the gas pedal to the floor. The sun was now starting to set and its bottom half was hidden by the horizon. The road was rapidly ascending up the mountain side and I started to think that it might be too late. The farther I went the more worried I became. Would I be able to find the spot in the dark? Even if I did, I would have to set up the tent using my headlights and I wasn't very keen on the task. I was steadily becoming convinced that my idea to come here was a bad one, and that finding a place to camp before dark was unlikely.

Just then it started to snow, and hard! The flakes were large and close together. I slowed down, and fear quickly began to rise within me. I could hardly see where I was going. And this was a dangerous road to say the least. It ran along the side of the mountain and there was no barrier to protect me from tumbling off of the edge. It was an accident waiting to happen, and with my luck, we wouldn't be waiting very long. To my left was a wall of stone that rose extremely high and steep, to my right was a drop off practically straight down for maybe four or five hundred feet!

Creeping along the road, I wondered what I should do. If I headed back then it would take longer and probably be even more dangerous than if I just tried to find a spot to stay the night. My hands were tense on the steering wheel and shivers ran through my body. I was scared. Suddenly, I could see a guardrail directly ahead of me. I realized that it was a turn in the road to the left.

Then it happened. The instant that I saw the guardrail I turned to see headlights coming straight at me, and there was nothing that I could do to avoid it. It was a big, old Mack truck. The driver must not have seen the turn either, because the truck gave no sign that it would stop. It ploughed into the back of my truck, sending the back of my truck through the guardrail. The front of it held onto the edge for an extra second, but soon fell through.

Petrified, the fall lasted for about four or five seconds and I was flipping end for end. The truck was airborne and with each split second its speed increased dramatically. The last thoughts that went through my head were how I never got to say one final goodbye to Sharon, or any of my friends. Nobody knew how much I really cared for them, and here I was about to die.

When I hit the bottom there were trees, but nothing substantial enough to stop the truck. So I rolled down the steep slope, hitting several small trees along the way. Then I finally hit a large tree that did stop the truck, but when this happened everything went black before my eyes. I was sure that this was the end of my life, but somewhere amidst this bleak picture, lay a tiny splinter of hope.

CHAPTER 2

My eyelids popped open with a crack, and I could feel the cool air rushing in to greet my waking eyes. I could see ceiling tiles above me and felt the comfort of a bed beneath me. I knew that I was in the hospital, but all I could think about was Sharon. I had truly thought that I was going to die and I couldn't bare the thought of leaving her. I had to tell her what happened, and that somehow I had miraculously survived. I tried to lift my head to look around, but felt a sharp wave of pain run through my arm. I laid my head back down on the soft pillow and tried to gather my thoughts. How did I survive that fall, I wondered, and how did I get to the hospital? I wondered if perhaps the driver of the truck had not been injured too severely and had responded quickly to my desolate situation.

I lay there staring at the ceiling for maybe another half hour, while turning these thoughts over in my mind. Surely someone must have swiftly come to my rescue, but it was such a treacherous terrain. Perhaps I was airlifted out of the valley by a helicopter. From what I could recollect, I felt that there was little chance of my survival, or that they would even find my truck.

The remembrance of the horrific accident was still fresh in my mind when suddenly I could hear footsteps coming towards my room. Someone was coming and I thought that hopefully I would finally be able to get some answers. I needed to know just exactly what had occurred and who else was involved.

A man walked into the room and came right up to my bed. He stood above me and stared directly into my eyes. He was an older man with greying hair, but he seemed exceptionally healthy for his age. A smile drew across his face.

"How do you feel?" he asked in a low, soothing, and almost hypnotic voice.

"Sore and dehydrated," I replied.

"Here, I'll get you some water." He left the room, and quickly returned brandishing a cold glass of water. I held up my hand and grasped the cold slippery glass. I tried to lift my head to drink from it, but once again felt the wave of pain in my arm. I could not even quench my own thirst and it made me feel rather helpless.

"Oh never mind it," I said. "Just tell me what happened."

"Well, as far as I can tell, you quite remarkably suffered only a broken arm," he said, and then paused for a second, "but it could have been a lot worse."

"Yeah, I know that, I thought that for sure I would die," I said a little bit sarcastically, as I felt that he was simply stating the obvious.

"Well, you don't know the full story yet," he said, "because apparently you did die." I jerked my head up to look at him, and gave him a confused look.

"What do you mean, I died?" I said.

"Just that," he said. "You were dead for a period of time. You see, what happened is that after you went over the edge of the cliff, the driver of the other truck called 911. I guess he wasn't too badly hurt, but apparently he had bumped his head on the steering wheel. I wasn't the one who checked him out. Anyway, there were no roads near where your truck had fallen and as a result it took us nearly two hours to get you. Luckily for you, an old friend of mine lives down in that valley and she had witnessed the accident from down below. As soon as she saw the accident, she went to the scene and there you were still inside of your truck. Now fortunately she used to be a nurse at this very hospital, and she was able to do First Aid on you." He stopped for a moment, and took a drink of the water that I had requested.

"Now like I said before", he continued. "You were dead! She said that you were not breathing and you had no pulse. Therefore, you were clinically dead, but she didn't give up on you. She began to perform CPR on you almost immediately upon arriving at the scene, and she continued doing CPR for twenty three minutes before you came back to life."

I was staring at him intensely, and feeling completely overwhelmed by this incredible story of my own rescue. "Wow," I said, "I'm one lucky son of a gun, aren't I?"

"You're damn right you are," he said sternly, as he stepped back after the heroic tale. He walked to the end of my bed and looked out the window. He seemed to be deep in thought and somehow affected by my experience. "Now, I am only a doctor," he said, "and I don't go beyond death." He turned back towards me, and looked me in the eyes. "But for one reason or another, you came back." Then he turned, and walked out the door.

Awestruck, it was all too much to take in at once. I had no idea what to think or feel. My mind went numb. A million thoughts were rushing through my head, but I couldn't focus on any of them. I had faced my own mortality, and lived! Yet I couldn't remember any of it. My head felt fuzzy. All I wanted to do was clear my head, but I knew that wouldn't be happening any time soon.

There was something extremely peculiar about this experience in addition to the fact that I fell off a mountain and died. The entire experience felt like a solitary of confusion and I knew that I had to eventually figure it out. It was inevitable,

17

but I wanted answers sooner rather than later. I wanted to put an end to this horrible dream, and just go home in peace.

Suddenly, the footsteps of another person entering the room caught my attention. A young woman walked in. She appeared frivolous by nature with vibrant, red curly hair and a bright, sunny smile. Her walk had a bounce to it, making her curly hair act like springs. For my foggy mind, it was quite funny to look at, and I had to suppress my laughter.

"Hi, I'm Nancy, your nurse," she said with her eyes gleaming with excitement. "How are you feeling?" I couldn't help but smile, just being in her presence was making me feel better. I looked away and thought for a second.

"Oh, I guess I can't complain," I said. "I mean, considering what happened it's a miracle that I'm still alive."

"I know," she said. "Some of the girls in the lunchroom told me the story. It sounded pretty amazing how you were saved, but you must have been scared. Were you?" She was looking at me with sincerity in her eyes.

"Yeah, I was really scared," I said. "I couldn't believe my eyes when I saw the truck coming towards me and I'm still kind of freaked out by the whole thing. Just the fact that I was dead is scary enough, and for twenty three minutes at that." She tilted her head and gave me a compassionate smile.

"Hard to believe you came out of it with only a broken arm! We'll help you get that fixed up easily enough", Nancy said. "It never ceases to amaze me how resilient the human body is. There have been some pretty remarkable stories of people who have been brought back by CPR. The hospital chaplain is available to talk to if you'd like. In the meantime, is there anything that I can get you?"

"Yes," I said, because I knew full well what I wanted. "I want to call my girlfriend. Is there a phone that I can use?"

"Of course, there is one here beside your bed," she said, while picking it up off a small table and setting it on my chest.

"I'll get out of your hair for a bit and give you some privacy."
She walked out, closing the door behind her.

I watched her as she left, admiring her helpfulness. The
phone felt heavy on my chest, and I wondered what I would
tell Sharon. I didn't want her to get upset, but at the same time I
wanted her to know exactly what happened. Death had almost
taken me away from her forever, and that was an unbearable
thought. I dialled the number, but I was still unsure of what I
was going to say. It only rang twice, and Sharon answered.

"Hello," she said, her voice suggested that she had just
woken up.

"Hi Sharon, how are you doing?" I said, trying to sound as
normal as possible.

"Oh Mike, hi," she said in the midst of a yawn, "I thought
you were going camping, are you out in the woods now?"

"No Sharon," I said. "I was in an accident and now I'm at
the hospital."

"What?" she said, her voice now more serious. "Oh my
God, Mike, are you okay?"

"Yeah, I'm fine, just a broken arm." Pausing, I tried to think
of what to say next. "But I almost died, Sharon," I said, as I
decided not to tell her that I did die.

"Oh my God, what happened?" she exclaimed.

"Well, when I got up to the mountains a snowstorm came.
I was creeping along the road and a truck came around a turn
and hit the back of my truck." I stopped for a second and then
she suddenly spoke up.

"Well I'm glad you're not seriously hurt, but how did you
almost die?"

I hadn't expected her to think that I was done of my story,
but perhaps it would be better if she didn't know what really
happened. Now I had to think of something quick. "Oh, well,
it could have hit the front of the truck just as easily as it hit
the back. If the truck didn't turn at all then I would probably
be dead."

"Well, thank God that you're not, Mike," she said. "I don't know what I would do without you." A soothing silence followed her words.

"Sharon," I started.

"Yes, Mike?" she said.

"I want you to know that when I thought that I might die, the last thing I thought about was you, and how much I truly love you. It was more important to me that you know that than whether I died or not."

"That's sweet," she said. "I know that you love me Mike, and I can't describe how much I love you. Anyway, do you want me to come home, when will you be out of the hospital?"

"Oh no, that's alright, I should be out later on today," I said. "You can stay with Ruth, but I am going to miss you."

"I'll miss you too," she said. "And give me a call anytime."

"Okay, I love you babe."

"Love you too."

Once again we said goodbye, and silence filled the air. Now I felt better and reassured by the words of love that were exchanged. It gave me confidence that I knew I was going to need. There were things that needed to be figured out, and now I had the energy to do it all.

I set the phone down on the bed with my right hand and looked at the cast on my left. I realized that I hadn't felt the pain from it since the doctor had told me the story. I had been thinking about other things and hadn't noticed it. Just as I thought of it, the pain shot through me again. "Why is that?" I wondered. There doesn't seem to be any pain when I'm not thinking about it, but as soon as I think of it, there it is. I compared this to past experiences of getting cut at work and not feeling the pain until I saw the blood. Strange, I thought.

Five minutes or so passed, and then the door opened. It was Nancy, and once again her eyes were gleaming with light. She walked up and put the phone back onto the table.

"So, did you get a hold of her?" she asked, beaming with curiosity.

"Yes," I said.

"Well that was quick," she said. "Wouldn't you want to talk to her longer than that? I mean, after everything that happened."

"I didn't tell her the whole story," I said, "I guess I didn't want to worry her."

"Huh, well, if that's what is best," she said. "Then I guess it's alright, but I just thought that you would at least like to talk longer than that." She walked over to the windows and opened up the curtains. It brightened up the room substantially and made everything illuminate.

"Hey, do you know the lady that saved me?" I asked, as she turned around.

"No, but I know Dr. White does," she said.

"Dr. White," I said. "Is he the fellow that was in here earlier? I never caught his name."

"Yeah, that's him," she said. "I wish he would start introducing himself to his patients, he always forgets to do that. Anyway, I think her name might be Lucy. Apparently she used to work here, but I've never met her. That was before my time."

"I see, I'll have to go and thank her when I get out of here," I said. "When do you think that will be, by the way?"

"Ummm," she thought, "probably later on today, but I'm not sure," she said. "Dr. White will be back to see you in a little bit and he can fill you in. Is there anything you need for now?"

"Hmmm," I thought, "No, I think I'm pretty good, but thank you."

"Not a problem, just push this button if you change your mind." She held up a little remote with a red button that was attached to the bed.

"Okay," I said. She then gave me a big smile and left the

room. What a lovely nurse, I thought, as she left. She hadn't done a whole lot physically, but she had made me feel a million times better mentally. Her jubilant personality was contagious, and no one could remain depressed in her presence. She gave out only positive vibes. If everyone were like her then this world would be nothing less than pure bliss, but I supposed that would get pretty boring.

After a while my thoughts shifted away from Nancy and turned to the unknown lady who had saved me. I would definitely inquire about her to Dr. White. I hadn't thought that there were any houses in that valley, and it appeared to be only forest. There couldn't be too many houses down there anyway, because I could remember looking down there in the summertime. All I remembered seeing were trees and a small river running through them. My mind was occupied for about forty-five minutes with these thoughts, and then Dr. White entered.

"Hello Mike," he said. "How are you feeling now?"

"Well, I haven't felt my arm in a while," I said, "but I think that is just because I have so much on my mind."

"Ah yes, pain is a funny thing" he said, as he flipped through the papers on the clipboard he was holding. "I'm not sure if I even understand it myself, because it doesn't always hurt when it should. Sometimes my patients will feel nothing at all at times when they should be screaming with pain." He looked up from his papers. "Anyway Mike, you're free to go whenever you want. Although you will have to come back in two weeks to get that cast off." He turned away from me and started to walk out.

"Wait," I said, and he turned around. "Can you tell me how to find the woman who saved me? The nurse said that her name was Lucy and that you would know more about her."

He was staring right at me and his eyes shot open. A smile appeared on his face. "You are in for a treat, my friend," he said.

"She can teach you a lot about life, however, it all depends on how much you are willing to learn."

"What do you mean?" I said. "All I want to do is thank her for saving me." He squinted his eyes at me and then let out a little chuckle.

"She lives in a little cabin in the woods and it's kind of hard to describe how to get there. I'll write down the directions and leave them at the front desk for you. How does that sound?" Dr. White asked. I sat up in the bed and felt the pain in my arm again.

"Yes, alright, thanks," I said, while trying not to focus on the pain. "Hey Doc, can you call a cab for me now? I'm about ready to go home."

"Sure," he said, "not a problem."

Nancy helped me to find the front desk and get the directions that Dr. White had left. I had never been in this hospital before, so everything was new and unfamiliar. Every direction had endless possibilities. I would have been lost on my own. Nancy had been a great help and she wished me good luck as I walked towards the front doors. I glanced back to see her smile and wave me goodbye.

It was only a moment of waiting outside before the cab arrived, and I got in to find an overweight man about my age. He had short black hair and pale white skin. He was smoking a cigarette with the window down a crack, but the ventilation was poor. I almost dreaded having to breathe in. As he pulled away the smoke cleared and I took a deep breath of the fresh air. A few small clouds floated in the clear blue sky and the sun's intensity felt warm on my face.

"So, where are you headed?" he asked, breaking the silence.

"Kinlock Road," I said. "Do you know where that is?"

"Yeah," he said sharply, and then looked away.

I looked back out the window and stared at the trees going by. I was glad that he wasn't much of a talker because I wasn't in the mood for conversation. I felt relaxed and peaceful, but I didn't know why. Certainly nothing good had come out of my attempted camping trip, I thought. I leaned my head back and tried to put the whole experience out of my mind. I just wanted to go home and rest.

The next thing I knew, someone was shaking my shoulder and I jolted up. I had dozed off, and now the driver was asking me which house I lived in.

"It's the fourth house on the right," I said in a kind of mumble. I wanted to go back to sleep, and I decided to do just that when I got home. We pulled in the driveway and I paid him generously.

"Thanks a lot buddy," I said, as I got out of the car. He just nodded in return, and backed out of the driveway.

I awoke the next morning with the sun shining in my eyes. My arm felt more painful than ever, and I decided to get up right away. I started making breakfast, which was not an easy task with only one good arm. As I poured a glass of orange juice, I noticed the directions that Dr. White had given me, as they were just sitting on the countertop. I had almost forgotten that I had directions to this lady's house, so I decided to look at them over breakfast.

When I finished making breakfast I sat down at the table and read the directions. 'Lucy Crane', read across the top of the paper in large letters. In smaller writing below, all that it said was, 'Bear Creek Road, north side, white peace sign, follow the trail'. "Could the doc be anymore vague?" I thought. And what's with this white peace sign? There was no specific address, or any such thing. It was simply five pieces of information that would take me to a place that I've never been and introduce me to someone whom I've never met.

I thought about it over breakfast, and decided that I had to go there right away to check it out. It seemed strange to me the way that the doc had told me about her and my instinctive curiosity was driving me. I imagined an old lady sitting there with a crystal ball, claiming to be some sort of mystical being. She'd probably tell me my fortune and analyze my dreams, I thought. I didn't believe in that garbage, but it would be kind of funny to hear what she had to say. I called Sharon and asked to use her car and of course, she said yes.

I drove down to Bear Creek Road, which was about a thirty minute drive from our house. It wasn't a very nice looking road, I thought as I turned onto it. I had never been down this road before, and by the looks of it not a lot of other people have been either. It was a dirt road and I could see that potholes littered the way. Too bad my truck got smashed, I thought, but hopefully this road won't damage Sharon's car.

Looking to the sun, I figured out which way was north and kept my eyes locked on that side. There were trees all around me and it was thick bush that the sunlight could not penetrate. After driving for about two kilometres, I could finally see something white up ahead. As I approached, I could see that it was a large white peace sign carved out of wood and propped up against a tree. Beside it was a trail that went deep into the woods. It was about the width of a golf cart, so I had to park the car and walk.

When I opened the door, I was met by a fresh breeze and the sound of birds singing. It reminded me of how much I enjoy the outdoors, and the reason I had wanted to go camping in the first place. I started down the trail with a grin on my face. I figured that I may as well make the best out of going to see this lady.

Chapter 3

It wasn't more than ten minutes of walking down the trail before I could see some sort of structure rising high above the trees. As I got up closer to the structure, a separate log cabin came into my view. It was very neatly made with each log perfectly straight and notched to fit into place. The structure was a tower made out of logs as well and tied together with rope. It rose maybe sixty feet into the air, and I couldn't help but wonder what it was for.

There was maybe a quarter of an acre cleared out and it was growing with fresh green grass. There didn't appear to be anyone around, and I wondered if she was even home. I decided to just stand there for a moment, marvelling at the beauty of the area. After a few seconds, I noticed another trail on the other side of the cabin. The ground seemed to go steeply down in that direction, and I figured that the river must be down there. I started to walk in that direction when the door of the cabin swung open. I stopped in my tracks and looked over.

There stood a lady who instantly awed me with her beauty. She walked towards me with the softest smile that I had ever seen, and her eyes gleaming with light.

"Hello," she said. "Were you heading down to the river?"

"Umm, actually I believe I'm here to see you," I said. "You are Lucy Crane, right?"

"Yes," she said. "How are you feeling now, Mike? Let's take a walk down to the river."

Without hesitation, she walked past me toward the path that had prompted my curiosity. I quickly followed behind her, never taking my eyes off of her. She had long, straight black hair that reached down past her shoulders and fluttered with each step. Her strides were long and smooth, and I had to push myself to keep up with her. I cleared my throat, preparing to speak when she turned sharply and stared into my eyes. I struggled to gather my words.

"Umm, I wanted to thank you for saving my life," I said. "I'm not really sure how to make it up to you."

"Make it up to me?" she asked, while revealing a rather confused expression. "I didn't save you Mike. I know that you think I did, but in truth there is nothing to be saved from." She looked at me for a second longer, slowly smiled, and started to walk again. Standing there puzzled, I tried to make sense of what she had just said.

"Wait," I yelled when I realized that she was getting away. She stopped, and I ran to catch up to her. "What is that supposed to mean?" I asked, "That there is nothing to be saved from." She just smiled, and laughed.

"Never mind that now," she said. "We will discuss that later as long as you're not in a hurry. Are you?"

"Well, no, I suppose I'm not," I said. "My girlfriend is gone away for three weeks, so I guess that means that I can do whatever I want," I joked.

"Good," she said. "You won't mind staying for dinner, then?" I nodded in agreement. "Come on," she said. "We're almost at the river, and you are going to love it down here."

We walked along side by side, and it was only a moment before I caught the first glimpse of the river. Crystal clear water was dancing up and over large rocks scattered throughout the riverbed as the sunlight was sparkling in the splashes it made. As we approached the riverbank the trees opened up, as if they were curtains parting to reveal a timeless play. It was beautiful, and I wondered if Lucy was thinking the same thing. We stopped a few feet from the edge of the water, and I looked over at her. She was staring straight into the middle of the river. Her eyes motionless, yet somehow she seemed fully aware of everything around her, including me.

"Lovely, isn't it?" she said, her mouth being the only part of her body to move.

"It sure is," I said, while looking around for a place to sit down. Before I could find one I looked back at her, and she motioned me over to her.

"Come sit down over here," she said, and she walked over towards the trees. Nestled in amongst the branches of the trees was an old wooden bench.

We sat down, not saying a word. She appeared to be in a kind of trance, just staring at the river flowing. So I stared at the water as well, but couldn't help wondering what she was thinking about. After a moment I looked at her again, and now her eyes were closed. She appeared to be very peaceful, so I felt that I should not disturb her.

"What do you think of it all, Mike?" she said quietly, without opening her eyes.

"I don't know," I said. "What do you mean?"

"Well," she said. "The whole deal, everything. What do you believe?"

"Umm, can I think about what I'm going to say?" I asked hesitantly.

"Sure," she said. "Take as long as you need."

I knew that I was about to have a debate. I figured that she was going to give me some spiritual crap about God and Jesus, or something. I loved delving into debates about religion and philosophy because I felt that spiritual stuff was all bullshit.

There was no proof of God, or any of that mystical mumbo jumbo. Therefore it didn't exist. After what seemed to be only a few seconds, but was probably more like five minutes, I was ready to begin.

"Well, I believe in science, and things that make logical sense. I have no use for things that can't be proven. Blind faith makes no sense to me. I want to know the truth, and simply believing something doesn't make it so. Why do you ask?" I said this very sternly, and she looked at me, taken aback. I hadn't realized how intense I was when I stated what I believed in, but her body language let me know. I was, in fact, too intense, and quite possibly too certain of myself. A constructive debate could never follow such a stubborn, predetermined opening statement of beliefs. I had to be open, I thought, and give equal consideration to all possibilities.

"Wow," she said. "You're really sure of yourself," and then she laughed. This made me smile and I laughed too. "Okay," she said. "Can I ask you something about what you just said?"

"Yeah, sure," I said, "anything."

"What do you think is the logical placement of science within everything?" she asked. I was startled by the question, and could tell that this was going to be a tough debate. I thought for a minute, and yet another minute. For a very long time I have considered logic to be the basis of science, and felt very strongly about this. However, logic could potentially explain science in a new way, but it seemed unlikely. The laws of physics stand firm.

"Well, science can measure anything in the universe," I said. "And quite possibly explain why we are here and where we came from. I mean, these are important questions that everyone would like the answers to, and hopefully through science we will be able to find them. I actually have a theory about how life came to earth, if you would like to hear it." She looked away from me, and stared back at the water with that same peaceful look on her face.

"Sure, let's hear it," she said softly.

I took a deep breath and cleared my throat. She would be maybe the twentieth person that I'd told my theory to so far, so I knew how long it would take. Some people thought that my theory was total bullshit, while others thought that it might be true. However, the majority of them had no idea, and could not comprehend what I spoke of. It was far too complicated for their weak simple minds, and beyond the confines of their bleak little worlds. Hopefully Lucy wouldn't be of the same narrow minded type and perhaps she would provide me with some insight.

"Okay," I said. "This theory involves the Earth, Mars, and the moon. Right now, in their current state, the moon orbits the Earth, while the Earth and Mars orbit the sun. However, the moon wasn't always orbiting the Earth, and it is almost impossible that this was so. I think that its coming here was not a smooth landing and that it caused widespread destruction in doing so. Remember that this is only a theory and that I don't have the means to go and prove that any of this actually took place". She looked over at me, and laughed.

"Don't worry", she said. "I won't lose any sleep over it. Go ahead, and continue." "Alright," I said. "So anyway, there is geographical evidence on these two planets and one moon that a major event has taken place between them. First of all I'll talk about the moon, which is interesting enough in itself. The moon is actually understood to be older than the Earth, so if this is true then it would be impossible that the moon has always been orbiting the Earth. It is also a known fact that its orbit is getting further away all of the time.

So the moon at one point had to come from somewhere else to orbit the Earth, and this would have been a shock enough in itself. It is a sixth of the size of the Earth, and that's pretty big. I think that there is more to this story though and that there were collisions involved. Partly, because there is a geographical discontinuity on the moon, being that there is a large piece of its spherical shape that is missing. I think it is at the South Pole, but I'm not quite sure.

Anyway, so if the moon wasn't always orbiting the Earth, then it must have had its own orbit around the sun, or possibly around another planet. It may have had a highly dysfunctional orbit through space, and it could have possibly come from a whole different galaxy. It was a space rock with its own arbitrary orbit, and subject to the gravity of any passing matter. It could have been sling-shot around another planet, who knows?" She had her eyes closed now.

"Are you still listening to me?" I said, rather boldly. She looked over at me.

"Yeah, I can picture it in my head," she replied. "So what happened next?"

"Well, do you believe that there used to be life on Mars?" I asked.

"Yeah, I recall reading something about Mars one time," she said, "I guess they have photographs of ancient cities and pyramids on Mars."

"Yes, that's right!" I said, as I was getting excited to see that she at least had a little bit of interest. "Okay, so picture Mars a few billion years ago, as a planet that is thriving with life. Similar to the abundant life that the Earth fosters in its present day, but this is Mars that we're talking about here. What I think happened is that the moon came along at a high speed and an irregular orbit. It then struck Mars, well, actually more like grazed Mars.

I think this because on Mars' surface there is what looks like something grazed it, and it is really huge. It's called the Valles Marineris, and it simply looks like a huge gash on Mars' surface. In the middle of this gash there is a large crater, and I think that it may have been the moon that made this gash. This crater in the middle would have been where the Moon dug too deep and it lost part of itself.

Now, because of the moon's speed in relation to Mars and

the physics of the collision, I think that the moon kept on going, and so did the piece that broke off. They kept on floating out into space and did not give in to the gravity of Mars. Of course, it would have slowed down quite a bit after striking Mars and this is how I believe that we then acquired it. It was slowed down enough to be caught by the next planet in line, Earth.

Also, think about how much water and atmosphere that would have trailed the moon after colliding with Mars. It would have stripped Mars clean, and took almost everything above its surface with it. Now, if the moon then proceeded to come into our orbit and make an orbit that would last, everything in its trail would succumb to the gravity of Earth. The Earth would be showered with the essentials of life, but for the piece that broke off the moon.

If it fell to the Earth, then it would leave a mighty big crater, and I think that I know where it is. If you look at the map of the world, Greenland is kind of centered between all of the continents. Greenland to me looks like a big crater that filled up with water and then froze. It looks like a collision crater that shattered Pangaea into the tiny fragments that we know today.

So I guess my theory would be that the moon came along out of nowhere, and snagged Mars' water and atmosphere which contained the nutrients of life. Then it swung by the Earth and showered us with life-giving nutrients. However, also delivering a nasty surprise that almost shattered the earth, not to mention the mess that it left Mars in."

She leaned forward in her seat and looked at me. "That's quite a theory you've got there Mike, and I am impressed with your pure desire to find the origin of man. You sound as if you sincerely want the answer, but I'm afraid you are looking in the wrong place."

"So, do you think that my theory might be correct?" I asked, feeling like a schoolboy waiting to hear my grade.

"Oh, I don't know," she said, "maybe it is, and maybe it isn't. It doesn't make much difference to me either way. Whether or not that took place isn't going to change my world in any way, but my question is, why does it matter to you?"

"Well," I said, stumbling for my words. "Don't you think people should know, and find proof that this took place? I mean, it will open up a new chapter of history to research and record. Does this not mean anything to you?" I stopped for a second, eagerly awaiting her response.

"Well," she said. "If you did go out and prove your theory, what good is it going to do you, or anyone else? How will all of this information help you to get through your everyday life? How is this theory going to help you to find happiness and lasting peace? How is looking out there going to help you to find yourself?"

"Myself!" I said. "I'm supposed to be looking for myself? Since when am I supposed to be looking for myself? I am right here, and that is all that I need to know."

"Exactly," she said. "That is all that you need to know. So why does it matter what may have happened a few billion years ago? You are right here, and you are the man for whom you seek origin. The answer must lie within you."

I thought for a minute, thinking that she might have a point. The origin of myself and the identity that I assume is worthy of finding. Perhaps it is the only thing that is worthy of finding, I thought. My existence will cease in death, as surely as the sun will set, but on the other hand the sun never really leaves. So perhaps my existence does not depend upon my body. Somehow this concept still seemed illogical to me. She seemed to be implying that the logical eventually converges with the spiritual, and that science has to be put aside entirely. It was too soon for me.

Suddenly she stood up and turned towards me. The sun glowed from behind her flowing hair. It appeared like something from a Hollywood movie, only all of my senses were watching and feeling these beautiful surroundings. I could not have been in a more thought provoking place, nor could I ever find a better time. But unfortunately our session was over, and it was time to leave.

"Let's go and grab something to eat," she said. "After dinner I want to talk some more."

Then she smiled and started walking towards the path from where we had come. I stood up, stretching my legs and back. I hadn't realized how long we had been sitting there. The sun was now beginning to sink and the shadow of the trees cast a shade over the river. It was truly remarkable. Somehow, my terrible accident had brought me to a beautiful forest and also introduced me to a wonderful lady. I felt as if things were getting better with each passing moment and that I was on the verge of an awakening.

Chapter 4

As we walked back up the path, the air felt cool on my arms and the thought of the warm cabin ahead felt comforting. Lucy walked along looking straight ahead, revealing no expression. I felt that I was safe with this lady, even though I didn't know anything about her. She seemed to genuinely care about my well being, which was evident in her modesty towards saving my life. Some people would expect something in return, but she didn't seem to care about material goods.

As we came into the clearing where the cabin was, once again I noticed the wooden tower. This time I noticed that there were two levels, and that the first level seemed to be attached to the trees. It looked like walkways extended into the woods like a spider's web. It was something that I had never seen before and the overall design was completely foreign to me.

"Hey, what is that tower for?" I asked her, as she was heading for the cabin.

"Well," she said. "I'm going to go put some food on. Why don't you go and explore it? You'll know what it is for whenever you see it."

"Okay," I said, already walking towards the tower. She

went into the cabin and closed the door. I climbed up the wooden ladder and couldn't help but marvel at the delicate craftsmanship. There was not a single nail, or any noticeable piece of metal on the entire structure. Everything was tied with rope, and the logs of the first platform were all perfectly notched to fit into place.

I reached the first platform and was amazed at what I saw. Walkways did extend into the forest like a web, except they now had an obvious purpose. On either side of each walkway there were vegetables growing. There were tomatoes, corn stalks, and even carrots. It was incredible how they were suspended up in the air like this, being almost level with the foliage of the trees. They could reach the sunlight up here, and even compete with the tree leaves for sunlight.

I started walking down the main walkway and wondered if anyone else had ever grown vegetables this way. The soil was cupped inside birch bark that formed a half circle, and was supported by two logs underneath, and then two more on either side. The soil just sat inside the birch bark and appeared to be very rich with nutrients. I had never seen anything like it, but why was so much effort put into gardening above the ground, I wondered. Then it occurred to me that she must be a tree lover, and this method meant that the land didn't have to be cleared.

Just then I noticed something off on one of the furthest walkways, and it looked like marijuana. I could almost smell the stuff, and as I walked over I was quickly met by the powerful stench of the herb. So that's why she's so peaceful, I thought, she's an old pot smoking hippie. She must have taken their way of living seriously, and that generation of beliefs to the extreme. Saving trees and getting high.

I had tried smoking that rotten stuff back in high school, but got tired of that whole scene pretty fast. I was not one of those kids who came to class stoned, and laughed at everything that wasn't funny. None of that nonsense was for me. I would much prefer to sit back and drink a beer. Oh well, I thought, everyone's got their own preference. I guess she kills two birds with one stone by doing this. She hides her illegal plants, and saves the trees simultaneously.

I found myself in a daze while just staring at the intricate design on the marijuana leaf and contemplating its purpose of existence. Mother Nature sure knows how to create artwork, I thought, but why did she have to destroy millions of minds in the process? I looked back at the tower, and remembered that it went up another level. "I wonder what kind of crazy shit is growing up there", I thought. I started walking back towards the tower, but suddenly Lucy opened up the door to the cabin below.

"Hey Mike, come on down and have a bite to eat," she yelled.

"Sure thing," I called back, feeling a little disappointed that I had to wait until after dinner to see the top level. I climbed down the ladder. She was standing in the doorway of the cabin.

"So what do you think of my garden?" she asked.

"Very nice," I said. "I see you've got some illegal substances up there." She laughed as she held the door open for me.

"Yeah," she said. "I like to smoke a little bit of the herb from time to time." I stood inside the doorway, looking around. There was a counter with cupboards above it, a woodstove, a bed, and a table. There was nothing new, or even relatively modern about the place. It was just a small little cabin, and probably no more than twelve feet by twelve feet. Nice and cozy like. There was a wooden peace sign hanging above the table, and it was painted white.

I sat down in one of the two chairs that were by the table and made myself comfortable. She was over by the stove cooking something that smelled delicious, and the smell alone seemed to increase my hunger. There was a bowl and a spoon in front of me, so I assumed that we were having stew or soup.

She came over and served me a thick, chunky, beautiful smelling stew. The aroma made my stomach growl, and I dug in right away. She sat down and cut me a slice of bread from a loaf on the table.

"So, did you build this cabin and that tower out there?" I asked, letting my curiosity disrupt my eating.

"Heavens no!" she said. "I could never build something that good! My father built this place about twenty years ago, but only after I was old enough to live on my own. I was the only reason that he didn't build it earlier. My mother died when she was giving birth to me, so he had to raise me all by himself. There was no way that he could raise a little girl out here in a place like this, but this is where he really wanted to be."

"I'm sorry to hear about your mother," I said.

"Don't worry about it," she said. "It was all part of the overall plan. Everything happens for a reason."

"Yeah, everything happens for a reason," I thought. It stirred up the memory of the old man at the liquor store. I was very angry at the time, but it turns out that he may have been right. If my accident had never taken place, then I never would have met Lucy, nor have found this beautiful place.

"So anyway," she said. "Three years ago he started getting weak, and he was no longer able to look after himself out here. He was barely able to get water from the river and he could no longer climb the tower. It was a dire situation, but of course it had its purpose. It was at the same point in my life when I needed a change, because nursing at the hospital was getting to be too hectic for my liking. So basically, we decided to swap places. He took my apartment in town, and I decided to stay out here."

"I see," I said. "Must have been quite a change of lifestyle, eh?"

"It sure was," she said, as she finished her stew.

"So where did your father get the idea to grow vegetables up in the trees?" I asked.

"I have no idea," she said. "He was always saying that people should live one with nature and not contribute to its destruction in any way. He was always doing things that were environmentally friendly, and sometimes he would even plant trees in his spare time. I guess this garden of his is simply a way to grow food without destroying the trees."

"So did your father smoke grass too, or was that your addition to the garden?" I asked. She laughed and threw her hair back.

"Yeah that was my addition," she said. "My father liked to drink every now and then, but he didn't like the weed too much."

"Does he know that you smoke it?" I asked.

"Yeah, he was alright with it though," she said. "I can be very persuasive, so I let him know that it's not that bad. Hey, speaking of weed, I'm going to go smoke a joint after you finish your stew. Do you smoke it?"

"No" I said, "but I don't mind if you do."

She laughed, "Well that's good, because I'm going to smoke it whether you mind it or not." She laughed again, showing me that she was only joking around. She got up from her seat and put her dishes away. I slurped up the last of my stew when her back was turned, as to finish up while still maintaining my manners. Then she came back and grabbed my dishes.

"So are you ready?" she asked, "It's almost time to go."

"Almost time to go," I said. "What do you mean? Almost time to go where?"

"We're going to go up to the tower to continue our discussion. I want to be up there when the sun is going down, it is kind of a tradition," Lucy said. I stood up and walked to the window that faced in the direction of the river. The sun was behind the trees, silently sneaking towards the horizon and preparing to leave us for the night.

"What do you mean that it is kind of a tradition?" I asked

her, while just staring at the trees as she finished clearing the table.

"Well," she said. "For the seventeen years that my father lived here, he always watched the sunrise and the sunset. He would be up on the tower every time, unless it was raining, snowing, or just too cloudy to see. He would often say that the sun was the giver of all life, and he was fascinated by its simple presence. So I do my best to experience the ritual myself, but I'm not nearly as self-disciplined as he was. Sometimes I forget about it. Come on, let's go!"

She walked out the door and I followed close behind. We walked to the tower and started to climb the ladder. Once again, I noticed how the first level was almost level with the top of the trees, and that the top level was well above all the trees. This structure must have been of great significance to Lucy's father, I thought, because of the amount of work involved in building it. It must have taken years.

When we reached the first level, Lucy jumped off of the ladder and onto the wooden platform. She walked to the corner where there was a steel water tank that I had not noticed before. It was suspended with boards that joined the tower to the trees and a little higher up than the first level. It was an old steel tank, and rust covered its surface. She pulled a lever that was attached to a hose which extended from the tank. There was a network of hoses that ran along the walkways up above the plants. After a couple of seconds water started to drip all over the plants, like a sprinkler system, only it was gravity fed.

"Nice," I said. "It makes life a lot easier." She shut off the lever.

"Yeah," she said, "let's keep going." We continued the climb up the ladder, rising high above everything until we reached the top. There was one wall that rose maybe four feet high, and a wooden bench along it. I looked around, being careful not to get too close to the edge. I was a little bit nervous of the height, especially since there was no railing. She sat down on the bench.

"Take a seat," she said. "I won't bite." I sat down beside her, and just marvelled at the landscape. The sun was maybe twenty degrees from the horizon and it cast a yellow shade across the treetops. The mountain looked huge from here, and its shadow stretched for probably a mile or two. The river cut through the trees, zig zagging all the way along the valley. It was beautiful up here, and I thought of Sharon, wishing that she could see this place. Lucy changed her gaze from the scenic beauty over to me, and I noticed her looking at me out of the corner of my eye.

"So does that mountain look familiar?" she asked.

"Yeah, that's where this happened," I said, as I was holding up my cast.

"Can you see the road from here?" she asked, and I looked closely. It was hard to see, but nestled on the side of the mountain there appeared to be a ridge that must be a road. I could faintly see a car, or at least the roof of a car, reflecting shimmers of light.

"Yeah, I think I can," I said, "just barely."

"Now, look down further," she said, pointing towards the far right edge of the mountain.

"Do you see on the corner there, where the guardrail is?" she asked.

"Yeah, I can see it," I said.

"Do you see where there is a little section of brand new guardrail?" she asked, "Because that is where your truck went over the edge, and I was sitting right here when it all happened."

I stared at the spot, remembering the horrible incident. The fear that I had felt was almost unbearable to think about. It had all happened so quickly, and it threw my world upside down in a heartbeat. Suddenly, I noticed how far away it was from us, and it dawned on me that Lucy must have walked all that way. There was no other way to get there, but through the woods.

"So you walked all that way through those woods just to save me," I said. "That must be at least two miles away, and you would have had to cross the river!"

"I told you before, Mike," she said. "There is nothing to be saved from, but yeah, I walked all that way just for you."

"Okay," I said, turning towards her. "You're going to have to explain this to me, because I'm pretty sure that you saved me from death." She looked me in the eyes.

"Mike," she said. "There is no such thing as death, only life exists, and life does not end."

I chuckled at the idea, and thought that it was rather absurd. Death is the end of life, and that is what almost happened to me.

"I don't believe that," I said. "If you didn't give me CPR, than I would be dead right now. It is as simple as that. I'm not trying to sound ungrateful, but I just don't understand your philosophy."

"Okay," she said. "I'm going to help you to change your mind about this subject, but I need a minute to think of the best way to approach it."

"Sure, go ahead," I said, but I knew that she wouldn't be able to change my mind. Death is as sure as the impending sunset, and there is no way to escape it. It is a fact of life, and something that we all must come to accept. She obviously believed in God or something, and there is no proof that God exists. I had no idea how she would attempt to change my mind, but it was less than a minute before she spoke up again.

"Okay," she said. "So you consider yourself to be a scientific man. Is that right?"

"Well, yeah," I said.

"Okay," she said. "Earlier I asked you a question that you didn't really answer. I asked you what the logical placement of science is within everything. When I asked you this, you gave me a big theory about how life came to Earth from Mars, which was your way of saying that you don't know. Now, I'm not saying that your theory is wrong, but I am saying that it is meaningless."

"Meaningless?" I said. "Don't you think that people should know where they came from?"

"Well," she said. "Even if it was true, it remains a very small aspect of a big and complicated answer. It opens up even more questions that will be even more difficult to answer. Such as how did life get to Mars in the first place? Now, I don't want to get into another big discussion about Mars and Earth, so let's just get down to the core of it all. Let's get down to the essence of all life.

Basically, we are having a debate about science versus spirituality, but there is no versus between the two if they are understood correctly. They do not contradict one another, but they must be looked at as they truly are. Not as two separate beliefs, but as one simple misunderstanding. Now, I'm going to try and save you some time, because whether you believe it or not, I've been through what you are experiencing. I know what it is like.

Growing up I didn't believe in God at all, and like you I thought that science had all of the answers. However, there remained a problem with this for me. Science comes up with too many answers, and none of them seem to mean anything. One could spend an entire lifetime researching one very small aspect of science, but still they would find more questions than answers. I didn't want to do this.

So I decided to look at the big picture, and try to find the foundation of the physical world. Somehow, I subconsciously knew that there had to be one true answer. There had to be one true answer that would put an end to all questions, and one that could not be contradicted. Of course, I did eventually find one, but the universe must first be looked at as it really is before the answer becomes acceptable. So let's talk about the universe for a little while. Tell me what you think of the universe."

She stopped talking, and was staring at me intently. It took a second to dawn on me that she was now awaiting my opinion. I was rather intrigued by what she had told me already, and clearly she understood the universe better than I. What could I say? What could I say to score one for the science world?

"Umm, well," I began, "I guess it all started with the big bang, and the universe has been expanding ever since. Eventually it will be drawn together again, because of gravity. Then I guess it starts all over again, and continues expanding and contracting forever. It is a vicious cycle that never ends, and we are just a by-product of this. At least that's what other people think," I said.

"What do *you* think, Mike?" she said, "because that is what I want to know. It will be difficult for me to help you if I don't know where you stand." I looked out to the scenery, which was even more beautiful than it was before. I wasn't sure what to think anymore. I thought that I had been getting somewhere with my theory, but maybe she was right. Even if I did find it to be true, it is still a small aspect of a huge answer. The universe is so huge, and no one person can understand the whole thing.

"You know," I said, "I'm not really sure what to believe anymore. There is so much out there that we don't know about. There is so much that we are yet to explore, and experience." I was hoping that she would tell me her thoughts, because she seemed as though she was building up to something. I was hoping that whatever she told me next would make sense, and that I could understand it.

Suddenly, she pulled out a large joint from between her breasts and put it into her mouth. Then she reached underneath the bench where there was a small box and she reached in to retrieve matches. She lit the end of the joint and took a long puff that accelerated the burning. She exhaled, and a cloud of smoke drifted towards me. The smell of marijuana was almost overwhelming and I had to lean back, as to avoid breathing in the toxic smoke.

"Are you sure that this doesn't bother you?" she asked, as she noticed my reaction to the smoke. I couldn't dare say yes, after telling her that I didn't mind.

"No, not at all," I said. She took a few more puffs, and inhaled deeply again. "Alright," she said, as she exhaled a huge cloud of smoke, so thick that it obscured the scenery behind it. "So eventually during the course of your scientific thinking, you are probably going to wonder where the universe came from."

"Yeah," I said. "I guess that is the big question, but there has to be a scientific explanation. Some people just say that God created it, but that's not good enough for me."

"No," she said. "It wasn't good enough of an explanation for me either. That's why I used to believe in science as well, but eventually it all came down to a point. It came to a point where science could no longer answer the questions that I was asking, and what I was inquiring about was completely beyond its reach. The realms of time and space did not contain the depth, or even the capacity of what I was seeking. I spent most of my childhood thinking about the universe, but it never really made much sense to me, until I asked the most important question that one can ask."

"What was the question?" I asked, as I watched her take another huge drag off her joint. There was a pause.

"What am I?" she asked sternly, while looking right at me. I was gazing at the mountain, and almost instantly the scene looked more radiant. The question immediately prompted me to think about myself, and curiosity about my own thoughts and feelings came directly to mind. What were they in relation to the scene I was viewing? For a moment it seemed as if I was connected to everything around me, but it was a sensation that I could not explain. I felt as if I was in control of my own situation and not at the whim of shifting external forces.

"Now, of course the scientific conclusion that most people would come up with to this question is that I am a body," she continued, bringing my attention her way. "But when I talk about myself, I'm not talking about skin, bones, and flesh. I wanted to know what I am, as in my thoughts, ideas, and emotions. Basically, I wanted to know what the mind is, and what its functions are. I tried to find a scientific explanation for these things, but it was hopeless. I spent much time thinking about the nervous system in the body and what those sensory transmitters really are.

Our minds are something that is beyond the body, however, and beyond all that is physical. The mere idea that the mind is limited to the body is absurd, and so is the idea that the mind is limited to the lifespan of the body. It wasn't long before I started to consider the brain and all of its workings as just another form of energy that can be found anywhere in the universe. It all seems to be the same energy, but the forms vary."

"Hold on a second," I said. "So you're saying that all of our thoughts are made up of the same stuff as anything else in the universe?"

"No," she said, "not at all. What I am saying is that the body and all of its workings are part of the universe. However, our thoughts, ideas, and emotions are not part of the universe at all. They are centered in the brain within a spot that is not within time or space. The mind is within a spot that is infinitesimally small, and completely beyond the measurement of science." She took a final puff off her joint, and butted it out. "But that does not mean that our minds are limited to the body, or confined within the brain. I have heard of people actually astral projecting at the hospital. Where they can leave their body, and can look at themselves from the outside."

"Do you believe in that astral projection stuff?" I asked. "I don't believe stories about that."

"Huh," she muttered, as she was coming to realize the question. "It doesn't really matter to me," she said. "I have enough proof for myself; to me their stories are just added witness to the fact that we are not bodies."

Her face was serene, and her gaze was soft upon the now setting sun. Added witness to the fact that we are not bodies, I thought. Well if we are not bodies, than what the hell are we? Her outlook on life was like none I had ever seen. I had to get to the bottom of the way that she thinks, but obviously not tonight. The sun was almost completely out of sight, and the valley was growing with darkness.

"So what do you think that we are?" I said. "If you don't think that we are bodies." She laughed, and turned towards me.

"I can't tell you that, my brother," she said, "For it goes beyond all words and symbols. It is something that you must realize, and then accept for yourself. What I am going to do is to try to tell you what you are not, and so what you really are is all that will be left. Only if you want to, not that you have to. We can talk about this more, and I will help you to figure it out."

"Well," I thought for a second. "I can come back tomorrow. I've got nothing to do for three weeks, so I may as well come back to this beautiful place and hang out with you." She smiled, bearing her white teeth against the black back-round.

"That would be wonderful," she said. "You know I didn't save you so that we could be casual acquaintances. You owe me, so now you have to be my new best friend." I laughed, and it felt good to joke around, after talking so seriously.

"Yeah," I said. "I probably should be getting home before it gets too dark." We both stood up simultaneously, and I cautiously climbed down the ladder. It was dark now, and I had to feel for every step. I got off at the lower platform, as she was climbing down like nothing, so I let her go ahead of me for the rest of the way down. We got to the bottom, and I jumped to the ground.

"Do you want to stay here, Mike?" she asked. "You are more than welcome to."

"No thanks," I said. "I'd better go home and call Sharon."

"Okay," she said. "Well, have a good night then, and think about what we talked about."

"Yeah," I said, as I pulled out my little key ring flashlight. "I will see you tomorrow."

I walked towards the trail, and turned to see her close the door of the cabin. A faint light appeared in the cabin, and I figured she must be using a gas lantern. There were no electrical wires out here or any source of power. She's living her life as if it were the olden days, I thought, and somehow resisting the temptations of modern technology. It must take a lot of will power to live out here.

The walk back was treacherous, but not in any serious sense. I simply hadn't realized how narrow the path was, and branches seemed to come out of nowhere, only to strike me in the face. The bush was pitch black, and owls could be heard lurking somewhere in its cover. I wondered if I would encounter a bear, after all, I was in Bear Creek. Panic was starting to build within me, even though there wasn't any apparent threat.

Suddenly, the words came to my mind 'I am not a body', as if I were being told this telepathically. Just then the clearing of the road came into view, and I could see the hood of my car shimmering in the moonlight. As if by coincidence, my sanctuary had come just as I had this thought. It was captivating. I got in the car, and drove home with a feeling of comfort and peace. I felt as if there were something bigger going on here and that it was all going according to plan.

When I got home the house was dark and emptiness filled the air. It didn't matter; I was in a session of deep thought. Bewilderment would be the best word to describe this. There was a kind of mysticism that surrounded Lucy and her way of thinking. It was contagious. My scientific contemplations were now on the verge of something bigger, and my theories meant nothing to me now.

Lucy was entirely right that my theory was only a small piece to a very large and complicated puzzle. There is so much history to the human race, and it should not be of top priority to figure it all out. We should be looking to the time of now, and determine what is the best possible way to make the future better for everyone. I would much prefer to have a good idea about where we are going, than to re-examine where we've been, and dwell on the horrors that have continuously plagued our human history.

There was something that Lucy was telling me that could be used in the time of now and directly influence one's current experience. It seemed to be an alternative way of looking at life and the world that we have all become so accustomed to. I had no idea if her way was right, and I vowed to uphold my scepticism until I had a better understanding. It was the only logical manner in which to proceed. Her talking about the body being part of the universe got me thinking that I was pretty small, but there was still something meaningful about what she was telling me.

I sat there in the darkness of my house, pondering these things until the wee hours of the morning. It had been a long time since I had been up all night thinking, and on this night there was no limit of things to ponder. In fact, there was too much, and not enough time to cover it all. Finally, the twilight broke my train of thought, and the birds' announcement that a new day had begun came just as my weary eyes were closing.

CHAPTER 5

When I awoke it was noon. The day was at its peak, and here I was just rolling off of the couch. My arm was sore once again, and for some reason I had a terrible headache. I stumbled to the kitchen and swallowed some pain killers with a glass of cold water. I was in one of those rare, yet all too familiar states of being only half awake, and half asleep. The remembrance of the day before came flooding back to me in waves. It seemed like a dream, and for a moment I thought that it really was.

I remembered telling Lucy that I would go back and visit her again today. Right now I dreaded the idea, and desperately needed the comfort of my own solitude. I had an empowering intuition that she was going to tell me something important, but it didn't matter. I was simply not in the mood. My body was tired, and there was no one to blame but myself. I had slept on the couch, which almost guarantees aches on the morrow. I lay back down in spite of this, and turned on the TV.

I remained there, mindlessly watching the tube, and all the while procrastinating about my trip to Lucy's. There was nothing of interest on, but I watched it anyway. A children's show captured my disgust, as puppets were interacting with ordinary people. It was incredibly lame, and far more sugar coated than the shows that aired during my childhood. Somehow, over the years reality had been saturated to the point of non-existence, and all that was left was an idealistic view of the perfect world. It was sickening. Two hours of this nonsense passed me by, and then I decided to go.

There was no reason not to go anymore, and I knew that I would torture myself if I didn't. My mind would not allow it. So I hopped into Sharon's car and began my journey down to Bear Creek Road. My mood was lightening along the way, and my body was now well rested. I put down the window and felt the cool mountain breeze. Bob Marley was jamming on the radio, and here I was driving my girlfriend's car. It made me laugh, and tap my hands to the rhythm.

The music delivered such a positive vibe, and it seemed to reflect the very same vibes that I got from Lucy. There is definitely a collective vibration, I thought, as I pulled up beside the old peace sign. There is definitely something bigger going on here. I shut off the car, and stepped out to find another beautiful day. There was not a cloud in the sky, nor a single bug in flight. There was nothing amiss as I started my walk down that narrow trail.

When I arrived at the clearing, Lucy was coming from the path that leads to the river. She was carrying a bucket full of water towards the tower, and she had a great big smile on her face. She set it down beside the ladder and turned towards me.

"Hey Mike, how are you doing today?" she asked.

"Oh, not too bad," I said. "I guess that's one downfall about growing your vegetables up in the trees," I said, while pointing to the bucket on the ground. "You have to bring the water up there, and do everything manually."

"It's not entirely manual," she said, "Come over here." She grabbed the bucket and walked to the rear side of the tower against the trees. There was a pulley system that ran up the side of the tower to where the water tank was. The nylon rope that was used had a hook attached to the bottom. She put the handle of the bucket unto the hook and started pulling on the rope. The bucket went up and turned upside down above the tank. She then let the rope slide back through her hands, and it brought the empty bucket back to the ground.

"Not bad, huh?" she said, smiling as she took the bucket off the hook.

"Yeah, I guess your dad had it set up pretty nice out here," I said.

"Oh yeah," she said. "He tried to make things as easy as possible without using electricity. Although sometimes I really wish that there was electricity out here, but I'm getting used to it. I mean, people have lived for thousands of years without electricity, so it can't be that big of a sacrifice." She paused, and looked in the direction of the river. "So, what do you want to do today? Would you like to go down to the river again?"

"Yeah, sure," I said, and we both started walking in that general direction. "So I was thinking about what you were talking about yesterday," I said, "I was up all night actually, and I'm still a little tired now. Anyway, I came to the conclusion that I still don't really understand what you are thinking. I mean, I still don't exactly know what it is that you are trying to say."

"Well," she said. "That's good that you thought about it, because I'm going to tell you more today. How's your arm, by the way?" She stopped, and faced towards me.

"Good actually," I said. "It doesn't really hurt much at all anymore." She smiled, and looked into my eyes.

"That's wonderful Mike," she said, "You're a good patient."

"Well," I said, "You're a good nurse."

"Thank you," she said. "Alright, I'm going to run inside the cabin for a second, and then we'll go down to the river. I'll try to make things much simpler this time." She walked towards the cabin, and I started wondering towards the path. I could hear the water in the distance, and the sound gave me a refreshing sensation. The air was fresh and everything around me was perfectly natural. I was feeling much better now than I had been at home, and no wonder. Just look at where I was!

I found myself admiring the unique appearance of some wild mushrooms and their diverse color patterns. They stood apart from the background hue of the dying grass and the evergreen trees. Just then she came back and grabbed my attention. We began our walk down to the river, not saying a word. Once again, I was struck by the river's beauty as it came into view. For a moment, we just stood on the shore and marvelled at the magnificent creation that lay before us. Then we both found our way over to the same old wooden bench and sat down.

"Okay," she said. "I'll try to explain my understanding of this world as best as I can, but you must be open-minded about it."

"Sounds good," I said. "Let's heat it."

"Alright," she said. "Basically, to my understanding there is only one mind, which is all of our minds joined as one. Everyone's mind is joined in one identity of pure love, and no one is excluded from this. The mind that we are lives forever, and cannot cease to be. It is impossible that anything in this world can harm us, or threaten our existence. However, in order for this ideal reality to be true, it also means that the entire universe that you perceive is not really there. It means that the universe does not really exist and is no more than an illusion. This includes your body and everything that you may associate yourself with. Nothing within space and time is real, because it is subject to change.

Now, of course this idea seems fairly far-fetched, and especially so when people believe only that which they can see. They tend to make presumptions about the whole when they can only see the surface, and what they get is madness. However, one must consider the amazing functions of the mind. For example, do you ever have dreams?"

"Well yeah," I said. "I think that everyone has dreams. Actually I woke up this morning, and thought that coming here yesterday was just a dream."

"Well," she said. "That's because it was."

"Ha! You're crazy; there is no way that it was just a dream," I said, "You saw me here too. You were here, too!"

"So," she said. "Two people witnessed the same dream. Does that change the fact that it was only a dream, that it was not real?"

"I don't understand," I said. "How can you just call it a dream?"

"Well, just let me explain," Lucy said. "Alright, so think of a dream that you had before, and it doesn't really matter which one. Pick a dream, any dream."

"Okay," I said. "I got one." I remembered an absurd dream that I had as a child. I had come home from school and all my possessions from that time in my life were laid out on the front lawn. As if something terrible had happened, and I no longer had a home. I recall running around and trying to pick them all up in a mad rush. They were just colouring books and other kid's stuff, but they were valuable to me.

"Alright," she said. "So everything that you experienced within that dream was not really there. Everything that you saw was not really there beside your bed where you were sleeping. It would defy every law of physics if it was real, and so it had to be all in your mind, right?"

"Yeah," I said. "I suppose so, but isn't that just the brain? Doesn't the brain use excess energy to create an image, or something like that?"

"It's not the brain," she said, seemingly disgusted at my ignorance. "The brain is just a part of the body; it is the mind that has all the energy. The brain is just a pile of electrified noodles that makes our minds appear complicated."

"Electrified noodles," I said to myself, and laughing at the description.

"Pretty much," she said. "Think about that image that you said was created by the brain during your dream. It was an image of spatial distance that far exceeds the limited distance between your brain and your skull. Call it the brain if you will, but it was your mind that created that image. Your mind projected and perceived an external world that was not there.

I mean, think about it. You are lying there in the safety of your own bed, and then you fall asleep. Normally, it would be an instant before you wake, but not if you happen to have a dream. That same instant suddenly turns into a period of time in which you have a dream. Things seem to happen, but they do not really take place."

"Okay," I said. "So what are you trying to say?"

"Well," she said. "Do you agree that your dream was only within your mind, and that it never really took place?"

"Well, obviously," I said. "It could never have really happened if it was only a dream."

"Yeah," she said, "Exactly. So now let's consider that dream as a little bang, and let's apply this same concept to what is known as the Big Bang. After all, that is how scientists say the universe began. It is basically the same as the little bang, except that all of the little bangs are simply repetitions of the big bang."

"Hold on a second," I said, as I was starting to get confused with this analogy. "The Big Bang was at the center of the universe, and it had nothing to do with us. It was billions of light years away from here, and we didn't even exist at the time.

"That's where you're wrong," she said. "That is the common belief, but who is to say that we are not the center of the universe?"

"What?" I said, not believing what I was hearing. Everything that she was saying seemed crazier than the last, and it made no sense to me. "That's impossible," I said. "The Earth revolves around the sun, which revolves around the Milky Way. Then the Milky Way makes its way around a huge cluster of galaxies like itself, and that revolves around something even bigger. We are billions of light years away from being even close to the center of the universe!"

"Alright," she said. "Let's take a step back to the little bang that was your dream. Who was at the center of it?" I was stunned, and had no choice but to answer.

"I was," I said, almost reluctantly.

"Right," she said. "It was only in your mind, and no one else had anything to do with it. Well, I am telling you the biggest secret ever kept right now. It is the same with the big bang. The whole damn thing is one big dream, and you are at the center of it."

There was a silence that followed this, and there was nothing that I could say, even though I didn't quite agree with it. This way of looking at the world was completely foreign to me, but maybe it was just the way that every pothead looks at life. Maybe they all see their lives as no more than a fucking dream, and something that shouldn't be taken too seriously. I shouldn't judge though, I thought. After all, Lucy seems to be quite satisfied with this uncommon belief, and it seems to make her happy.

The silence lasted for maybe twenty minutes, but it seemed like much less. I was trying to make sense of it all, and she was just staring vaguely into the river. Almost as if she was patiently waiting for me to catch up, as she was done learning herself.

"So let me get this straight," I said. "You're saying that our experience of this universe is just one big dream!"

"Yes," she said. "For example, here is a simple explanation of this understanding. Let's take two separate yet equal experiences where one is rendered as a dream and the other is not. Such as that dream that you had, and five minutes after you woke up from it. Those are two separate experiences of which one you have recognized as a dream, and the other you think really happened.

You think that five minutes after you woke up is your real life. Whether you were getting dressed or eating your breakfast. You think that these things are really happening, and that it is as real as it can get. However, the dream that you woke up from five minutes ago is considered just that, a dream. Whether you just killed someone, or were getting hunted down yourself. It doesn't really matter what you did because that was just a dream, and those things didn't really happen. Do you see what I'm getting at here?" she said, looking right at me, and speaking with such sincerity. "Every single experience is different in appearance, whether it is a dream, or what people call real life. But the very fact that every single one is different makes them all the same. They must all be under one category. They all must be either real, or unreal."

"What do you mean? I said, "How can the fact that they are all different make them all the same?"

"Well," she said. "Every experience is different, and so that is one similarity. You see, all experiences seem to be of something external to you, but not of you. Yet you fail to recognize that the one who perceives is the one who projects. Just like the experience of your dream. What you perceived is what you projected within your own mind, and the dream was a simple illustration of your own thoughts.

Dreams are an example to us of the unreality in all experiences, because the laws of time and space are not upheld within them. For instance, five minutes after you awoke was your bearing that rendered your dream in the night as unreal, and you would have thought it was real if you did not wake. So with a logical mind does it not make sense to also question the reality of five minutes after you woke up as well? How real is the world in which we live?"

There was silence again. What could I say? There was no way that I could answer this question. I had no idea what was real anymore, or if anything was real. It kind of made sense to me what she was saying, but I couldn't understand it. There was no way that I was ready to consider this world as one big dream, but I suppose that it would settle a lot of debates if it was.

The conflicting evolution and creationism beliefs would merge together into one creating evolution philosophy, and scientists would rejoice with people of faith. The entire world would come together with one common understanding, and differences would not be seen. The dreamers would transcend the dream, and become one. It seemed a little too idealistic, but still I craved to know more.

"So if you don't think that this world is real," I said. "What do you think is?" She looked over at me again, and smiled.

"Us," she said. "You, me, and everyone else, we are all one mind. You see, a dream can never destroy the dreamer, and so it is that we are the constant. As everything changes, we stay the same. We are eternal beings that are perfectly capable of happiness within our own union, yet why do we fail?"

Once again I had no idea. I couldn't understand why everyone fails to be happy. It seems to be what everyone wants, including me, but nobody seems to be able to find it.

"I don't know," I said. "Are you happy?"

"Yeah," she said. "I am, and do you want to know why?"

"Sure," I said. "Maybe someday I can find happiness too." She looked at me.

"Of course you can find happiness," she said. "We all will, and it won't take very long. The world is becoming happier all the time, and it all has to do with the way that we are thinking. We have been evolving our thoughts and the dream simultaneously for thousands of years, and we are coming to a point now where a collective awakening is inevitable.

Let me tell you what happened to me nine years ago at the hospital. I had never lost a patient before this time, and had never really thought about what it would be like either.

Anyway, one night I was working late, and was getting ready to go home. Suddenly, a young woman burst through the door, she was about to have a baby. So me and the other nurses put her on a bed and called in the doctor.

This was also the first time that I had ever assisted in delivering a baby, and so I didn't really know what I was doing. I did whatever the doctor told me to do, but I pretty much just stood there the whole time. I watched from the sidelines as a beautiful baby was born into this world. It was amazing, and I was so happy. But just as I was getting excited, the doctor said that something was wrong.

There was nothing wrong with the mother, but the baby wasn't breathing the way that it should. The doctor took its pulse and it had an irregular heartbeat. I started to panic and get frustrated. I was thinking why did this have to happen? and I felt terrible. Anyway, a long story short, the baby died fifteen minutes after it was born and I was in a complete mess. I went into the waiting room and cried by myself. I was there alone until about three o'clock in the morning, and then a man came in.

He was one of the older patients, and I knew that he was fairly sick with cancer. He came in and sat beside me. I wiped away the tears from my eyes and sat up straight. He talked with me for five hours, and we didn't finish our conversation until the sun came up. He told me pretty much everything that I am telling you now. He told me that it is all just a dream, and that the baby never really died. Somehow, he was able to convince me of this, and from that day forth my life was different.

I contemplated what he had told me over the next several years, and it really made sense to me. I started to consider this world as just a simple dream, and that is what made me happy. To know that what I perceive is that which I simultaneously project. It meant that I could choose not to project that which I would rather not perceive. This makes fear disappear, and love return to sight.

Now, we are on the verge of something else here. Something much deeper, but I don't want to continue unless you are ready. So I want to hear what you think about what I am telling you".

"Well," I said, leaning back on the bench to stretch. "I think that you could be right, but to me this world is still very much real. I cannot conceive of the idea that this world is just a dream, it seems rather absurd. This bench is real," I said, as I slapped it. I could feel the sharpness of its rough surface.

"Okay," she said. "Well, say you have a dream about this same conversation tonight. Will you still think that it is real when you wake up?"

I stood up in frustration and walked towards the water, picking up a rock along the way. "I don't understand it!" I yelled back to her. I could see her stand up gracefully and walk gently upon the sand towards me. She put her hand on my shoulder and looked me in the eyes. It gave me a sense of comfort and peace.

"Don't worry," she said. "It will be alright." She then took the rock from my hand, and held it up in front of my eyes. "This rock," she said, "is an illusion. It is not really there, but you are."

"What?" I said amidst a state of confusion.

"Never mind," she said. "Hey, do you want to go for a canoe ride?"

"What?" I said, as I was coming out of my mind boggle. "You have a canoe! That's awesome! I'd love to go, I think my poor brain needs a break."

"Great," she said. "We will have to walk upstream a little ways, but its clear sailing from there. My father has a canoe up there, but do you want to go and grab a bite to eat first?"

"Yeah, I'm starving," I said, "but I don't want to eat all of your food. You should let me take you in town for dinner."

"Oh no," she said, as we started walking towards the path. "Don't worry about it. Besides, if we go in town then it will be dark by the time we get back, and I'm in the mood for a canoe ride."

We walked back to the cabin, and she made us some sandwiches. Then she climbed up onto the table and retrieved two paddles from up in the rafters. After that, we made our way back down to the river and followed it upstream towards the west. A rocky terrain made the walk treacherous, and there were a few times when I had to help Lucy. Then at one point, we came to what could almost be considered a waterfall.

As we walked up the steep embankment next to the waterfall, the scene of the river took a drastic change. This waterfall separated the river, as if it were acting as a dam. The rugged rapids of the river below stopped, and what started was amazing. The water was calm, and it reflected the trees like a mirror. It was at this same point that the only place to walk was through the trees, but luckily there was a trail.

"This way," Lucy said, as she walked into the cover of the forest. We walked along the trail until the sound of the rapids could be heard no more and the soothing sound of birds chirping took its place. Then eventually the river took a bend to the left, and it was here that the canoe was stationed. Leaning up against a tree was an old orange canoe, almost covered from the dropping foliage of the trees above.

"Well this is it," she said. "What are you waiting for? Put it in the water." I stood there looking at her, thinking that she was serious, but then she laughed. "I'm just kidding, Mike, come on, let's each grab an end." We both picked it up and brought it to the water's edge. She pushed it out into the water and held onto the end. "Did you ever do this before?" she asked.

"Once or twice," I said, "but that was years ago."

"Okay," she said. "Well there are a few things that you should probably know. First of all, once you sit down do not stand up, because I don't want to flip it. The lower your center of gravity is, the more stable the canoe is. Secondly, don't move from side to side, because again I don't want to get wet. Besides, we don't have any life jackets, and swimming isn't my forte."

"Don't worry," I said. "I'm a good swimmer, so I can save you if we flip it."

"Well you'd better," she said. "You owe me one life saving resuscitation already," she laughed. "Alright, you get in first. I want to be in the back, so that I can steer."

I held onto the sides as I climbed to the front of the canoe. I was trying to keep myself low and centered, but I could still feel the boat's unstable nature as I took each step. Finally I got to my seat and sat down very carefully. She got in quickly, without shaking it once. She then handed me one of the paddles and pushed us away from shore with the other. I waited as she paddled us out into the middle of the river and turned us towards the sun.

I put my paddle in the water and attempted the first stroke. As I did, the canoe went down on that side, and it became obvious that this would take a little practice. I had to hold the top of the paddle with my broken arm and try not to move it too much. I tried to lean the other way when I paddled, as to compensate for the balance. After a moment, I realized that my strokes were weak because of this. So I sat up straight and tried to paddle more perpendicular to the water's surface. I could feel the difference, and the canoe thrust forward with each new stroke.

"There you go!" Lucy said from behind me, and a smile drew across my face. I felt like I was getting the hang of it, and was really starting to enjoy the ride. Lucy seemed to be keeping a lower, more constant pace. I couldn't hear her paddling, and I looked back a couple of times just to see if she even was. Each stroke that she made hardly made a sound, and her turns were graceful. Meanwhile every time that I paddled, it made a loud splash and rocked the boat a little bit. At one point I accidentally splashed her, and looked back to see that she was laughing about it.

"You must do this a lot," I said. "You seem to be really good at it."

"Not really," she said. "This was more of my father's thing, but he used to take me out whenever I came to visit. I haven't really done a whole lot of it since he moved back into town." I stopped paddling, and it was silent again. Other than the birds, the only sound was a faint dribble coming from Lucy's paddle every few seconds. The scenery was amazing. The sun reflecting off the calm water kept its image a few feet ahead of us as we paddled. I was staring at the water with amazement. The water seemed foreign to me, and perhaps it was because I had never given it much thought. It seemed incredible how the water was holding us up, and how the boat was keeping us from sinking.

"Buoyancy is a pretty powerful force," I said. "If you think about it, I mean think of all those huge oil tankers out in the ocean. There are thousands of tons of steel being held up by water, and a lack thereof."

"Yeah," she said. "You know buoyancy is basically a reciprocal of gravity."

"What do you mean?" I said, before I even had a chance to think about it.

"Well," she said. "Gravity pulls things down, and buoyancy pushes them up. It is basically matter trying to find its neutral point. Such as if you held a ball above the water and dropped it. It would fall to the surface, which would be its neutral point. Similarly, if you held the same ball underwater and let it go, it would rise to the surface, which would be the very same neutral point.

Anyway, let's not talk about science, please. It seems foolish to me now, and it doesn't get you anywhere. I mean it when I say that the greatest achievement that science can obtain is to prove itself as unreal. That is all that it has done for me, and that is all that it can do for you." She stopped paddling, and the canoe gently slowed down. "Alright Mike," she said. "Without the universe, science does not exist, because there is neither time nor space in which it could exist. I am telling you right now that the universe does not exist, but you probably don't believe me. That's alright though, because it's all going to plan."

Just as she said that it is all going to plan, the memory of the old man at the liquor store came back into my mind. I had been a real asshole to him, and I wished that I could take it back. I wondered if Lucy knew who he was. They seemed to have the very same outlook on life and they share the same positive nature.

"Do you have an idea of what I'm talking about?" she asked.

"Not really," I said. "I need some more of the basic questions answered. I understand that you think that this is just a dream, and that everything that I see is not really there. But if this is true, then why are we dreaming? Why are we here in the first place? And what purpose could we possibly have? What is the purpose of dreaming this world?"

"I agree," she said. "It's not enough just to know that you are dreaming, but that is an important piece of information. It is also important to understand the origin of the dream and what set it into motion. There was no real purpose for the Big Bang, other than our own curiosity and foolishness. The dream was thought into motion, and we've been here ever since. Our only purpose here now is to undo those same old thoughts that continue the dream in little continuous bangs.

Let's use a nightmare as an example, during which fear is your main emotion. Now, how this dream took form is misunderstood. The average person would say that they were fearful because the things within the nightmare were scary. Whatever happened or whatever was anticipated to happen caused them to be fearful. However, this could not be more wrong.

What really took place is that they felt the fear initially, and this is what gave form to the dream. The fear is what they did project, as to put it into a form of which they may perceive. The nightmare was no more than an illustration of their own terrible thoughts. Any dream, as I may have mentioned earlier, is a little bang. It is a repetition of the initial thought that created the big bang and a means for continuation. It is sometimes hard to recognize, but when one observes the dream as well as the coinciding thoughts, things become much clearer. Why certain things happen is better understood. Our thoughts have a direct influence on our experiences. For example, I'll bet that your car crash was preceded by fear."

"You're right," I said, as I was amazed that she knew this. "I was scared that I would not find a place to camp before it got too dark. That fear may have caused my trip to the liquor store to get delayed. Then, the fear in me grew even more, and that's when it started to snow. And finally the fear grew really intense, and that's when it happened. That's when I was ploughed off of the mountain's edge and hurtled into oblivion."

"You see," she said. "Your thoughts coincided with the dream and fearful thoughts preceded fearful events. You allowed the fear to continue rising within you, until the point where something major had to occur. There was so much fear in you that it had to be extremely frightening and terrifying.

As for the fact that I brought you back into this world, this could mean that you also had some thoughts that were not based in fear. You must have consciously decided to come back, for reasons based in love. It is the only real reason to come back. There must be something that you are supposed to do or say."

"Wow," I said. "I don't know how you know that, but I think that you might be right. My last thoughts were of my wife and how much I love her. I wouldn't have been able to tell her this had I died, so perhaps it was my decision to come back. Perhaps it was my will to return to this world and tell her how much I care about her."

"I do not doubt it one bit," she said. "I am sure that you

made a lot of choices that you don't remember while you were dead. Including the choice to come here and talk to me."

"You think so?" I said with curiosity, as I turned towards her.

"Absolutely," she said. "Everything happens for a reason, and the reason is by choice. You do not go into any dream without the thoughts that create it, and these are your own thoughts. Only you can control them and choose which thoughts to have. However, these choices are often made subconsciously, so people do not realize that they have free will. They do not realize that they are in control of their own thoughts, and this is rather sad in my opinion."

"I see," I said very slowly, as we floated upon the still water. "It's all very interesting, but I'm finding it hard to wrap my head around all of this. These answers seem to be all too simple."

"I know," she said. "It is because I am introducing you to a whole separate way of thinking, and it is quite simple really. The only problem is that your old way of thinking was very complicated and confusing. Every answer had multiple backup answers, and none of them really answered anything.

It is a gradual process of unlearning the old way of thinking that you have taught yourself, and then our natural way of thinking takes its place. The whole world is experiencing this shift right now, but it is relatively gradual, so they do not see it. It is taking place behind the scenes, within the mind of every person on this Earth." She then took her paddle, and turned us around. "Are you ready to head back?" she asked.

"Sure," I said. "My free will is telling me to go to the liquor store and pick up some brews. I feel like getting really drunk tonight!"

"Oh yeah!" she said, laughing. "Well, my free will is telling me to go smoke a joint under the stars tonight. You are welcome to join me if you like." I looked back at the sun to see that it was sinking fairly low.

"Yeah, I might just do that," I said. "I'll go to the beer store and then come back here. We'll get drunk and stoned tonight, but is it all right if I stay here overnight? There is no way that I am going to drink and drive."

"Of course," she said. "Not a problem, and besides I'm not going to let you drink and drive after seeing what you can do while your sober." She laughed, "No, I'm just kidding, Mike. I shouldn't say that."

"You're cruel," I said. "Another remark like that, and we might just go for a swim." I looked back at her, and saw that she was smiling. She knew full well that I wouldn't dare tip the canoe.

From then on we didn't speak on the ride back. I was in another session of deep thought and not in the mood for talking. If Lucy was right about free will and I did choose to come back here, I must do something. Perhaps Sharon and I are supposed to get married, I thought. This would prove my love for her and make her happy. After all, she had always said that we should get married, but I kept telling her that we didn't need to. I am not really sure why, but I have always been reluctant to get married. Just the idea of being tied down, I suppose.

But whatever it takes I will prove my love for her, I thought, as we traversed that beautiful scenic river. Then suddenly, something occurred to me, and it seemed to come from nowhere. It occurred to me that even though Sharon and I were separated by distance, I could still feel her love, and I knew that she could feel mine. It was almost as if we were already married, only not officially. We were united in mutual love and respect.

It makes sense to me now, I thought, that this world must be only a dream. For how could my love for Sharon exist through distance, unless it was unreal? If this world were real, then she would have to be here in order for me to feel her love, but our love seems to transcend all distance. Our love knows no barriers, no limits. It is boundless. I was beginning to hope that

Lucy was right, because that would mean that we are already married. United as one, and separated by nothing.

Chapter 6

Before I had realized how far we had gone, we were back at the spot that we had departed from. The air was now getting cool, and the sun was nowhere to be seen. It was still bright enough to see, but the darkness was growing quickly. Looking into the cover of the trees was like looking into a void. We walked back to the cabin but didn't really talk much along the way. My thoughts were much more fluent than my voice.

When we got back to the cabin, she decided to stay there while I went to the beer store. So I put the pedal to the floor on Sharon's little car, and made excellent time. Everything went smoothly, and it wasn't long before I was back at Lucy's. I had bought her a bottle of wine, but I wasn't even sure if she drank. I knew that it wouldn't go to waste, though. I'd drink it if she didn't, but of course I also had a dozen beers for myself. I was good for the night.

I lugged the booze down the path with one hand as I shined the flashlight with my broken arm. As I was walking towards the dimly lit cabin I almost tripped over a stick and the bottles made a clatter. It was enough noise to let her know that I was there, and she opened up the door for me. There was a gas lantern hanging from the center rafter and it gave a soft luminance. I walked in and set the booze down on the table. There were three candles on the table as well, and they were all lit.

"That was fast," she said.

"Yeah, sometimes I like to drive pretty fast," I said. "I got you a bottle of wine by the way, if you want it. I wasn't quite sure if you wanted anything, but I got you something anyway."

"Sure," she said. "Thanks a lot." She went over to the cupboard and retrieved a glass and a corkscrew. "Alright," she said. "Let's do this thing," she laughed, and removed the cork. I cracked open a brew and sat down at the table. I leaned back on the chair and rested against the wall. She had a fire going in the stove, and the cabin was nice and cozy warm. She poured herself a glass and sat across from me.

"You know what, Mike," she said. "I think tonight's going to be a good night."

"Why do you say that?" I said.

"Well," she said. "First of all, this will be the first time that I've had anything to drink in a long time. I used to drink about once a month when I lived in town. I would get a few friends over, and we would have a blast. Secondly, you're here, and I have been really enjoying your company of late. I have some really good news, and I'm going to tell you about the incredible implications of forgiveness. I'm going to tell you everything." I laughed, and just thought that it was kind of funny for some reason.

"Sounds good," I said. "Once I have a few beers in me, I'll be ready to talk about that stuff all night long." I thought for a second. "If you had to put everything that you want to tell me into one sentence, what would it be?" I asked, and she looked into my eyes, speaking without hesitation.

"The foundation of the entire universe rests upon a silly belief that we had, and it simply was not true, Amen."

"Wow," I said, while trying to break it down in my head.

"Basically," she said, "I would tell that this world does not exist and that it is no more than an illusion of false thoughts. However, I am not going to dismantle your world and leave you with nothing at all. Not without at least giving you my assurance that there is something better, and that hope is justified. I am going to try to explain what this is, but it really goes beyond all words."

She stood up and walked to the cupboard. Then she returned with a cookie can and opened it up. Instantly the sent of marijuana filled the air, and she pulled out a small little bud. She sat back down and proceeded to break it up with her fingers. She must have done this a million times, I thought, as I watched her roll it into a joint.

"What do you say we go up to the tower?" she said. "It's always nice to be up there when the stars are out."

"Sure," I said. "Are you going to make this whole life thing make sense to me?"

"I sure am," she said, as she finalized her joint by putting a filter in the end. "At least I am going to try." Then she put the joint behind her ear and grabbed the bottle of wine. "Are you ready?" she asked.

"Yeah," I said, as I grabbed my box of beer. "Let's go!" When we got outside I realized that I could not carry the beer and climb the tower at the same time. So I had to think of something else, and I didn't want to ask Lucy to carry it. It appeared to be a difficult manoeuvre no matter which way I looked at it.

"Hey," I said to Lucy. "How am I going to get my beer up there?"

"Put it on the pulley," she said immediately.

What! I thought to myself, but was in the process of doing it anyway. I thought that it might rip the box, but it didn't. Everything worked out great, and Lucy was able to grab it from up above. After that, I climbed myself up to the top of the tower in the pitch black. Only the feel of the ladder let me know where I was, and I was a little bit nervous of falling. When I reached the top I looked up and could see the stars perfectly with not a cloud in sight.

I sat on the bench alongside Lucy, and lifted my head towards the skies. The Milky Way was marvellous and looked just like a white cloud that split the sky in half. I suppose that in a sense it is but a cloud, I thought. A googolplex of enormous fireballs of which our sun is but one. Amidst this madness our sun is only a spark on the outskirts of a raging fire, and in the presence of this fire our little blue planet seems rather insignificant.

Lucy noticed me looking to the sky, "What does all that mean to you?" She asked.

"Do you mean the stars?" I said, making sure that they were what she meant.

"Yeah," she said. "What do they mean to you?"

"Well," I said. "To me, they represent the fact that we are rather small and insignificant amidst the complexities of the universe. It represents how little we know, and just how much there is to know. We are a very small fragment of that great spiral of energy, and there is nothing that we can do to control it. Or at least that is the way that it appears to be. I could be wrong, though, because you're telling me that we are the center of the universe."

"That's right," she said. "Even though it seems to be as you described. It appears that way, because that is how you think of yourself. You think of yourself as rather small and insignificant amidst the universe, and so you project that image. You see everything as being outside of you and deprivation as all that lies within you. It is the greatest illusion ever created, and the saddest story ever told. In this world the stars are symbols of what we think we are which is separated; by distance and time.

However, what if the observer were to look at all of the stars as one? Would they not come together as a single universe?

It could be either billions of divided lights in the sky, or one single universe. It all depends solely on the perception of the observer, and it is the same with observing people as well.

We can appear as separated into millions of different human beings, or united as one single glorious being; as divided people, or as a God. Like I said, this depends entirely upon the perception of the observer. You can look at everyone as different people or as a united soul. However, unlike when we look at the stars, we can feel this unity. When we come together as one, we can feel our union, our love."

"I think that this is the first time that I have heard you use the word God," I said. "So you do believe in God, eh?"

"Yeah," she said. "But not in the traditional sense. I do not fear God like some people do, and I do not belong to any particular religion. I would actually rather not use the word God most of the time, because some people get turned off by it. Sometimes God is given a bad name by those who know not what God is."

"Well who does know who or what God is?" I said, "Nobody really knows!"

"That's not true," she said. "There are people who do know, but their voices often go unheard. They are still being obscured from the public eye by the older concepts and beliefs about God, which overwhelm the population through fear. The people are left feeling that they have no choice except to fear God's judgement, but I'm pretty sure that this is all changing. I am pretty sure that average person is beginning to see through the dream, and understand the true meaning of the word God."

"The average person!" I said, and I took a long drink from my beer. "Are you sure? Because I think that the average person is losing faith in religion and that less people are holding a belief in God."

"Yeah, I'm pretty sure," she said. "Because believing in God and having a religion is irrelevant to feeling God. There is a difference, you know. Believing in God is similar to saying that you think that He is there, but you're not quite sure. Meanwhile, feeling God is something that satisfies our belief and quenches our thirst for knowledge."

"Wow," I said. "So what is God? I mean if the average person is beginning to feel it, then shouldn't everyone know what God is?"

"Basically," she said, and then she took a sip of wine. "We are God. You, me, and everyone else, but God is not who we think that we are. God is who we truly are, which is infinite and eternal love."

"Okay," I said, almost not believing my ears. "So you are saying that we are God, and that we are infinite and eternal love."

"Yeah," she said.

"That's quite a statement!" I said, as I took another drink.

"Tell me about it!" She said, "But it's the truth, and a rather convenient truth, if I do say so myself."

For the next few minutes I sat in bewilderment. I could not deny what she was saying, but I had no proof of it as well. I simply had to trust that what she was telling me was true, and this is not an easy task, especially for me, someone who is sceptical about almost everything. Suddenly she started to speak again, and my ears instantly perked up with interest.

"What I just told you is the good news, but it won't really mean anything to you until this dream no longer means anything to you. So I'd like to go over the universe once again, but this time I'll start at the beginning."

"Okay," I said. "So that would be the Big Bang."

"Yes," she said, "But I want to start a little bit before that, because you may not know that such a time existed."

"So," she said. "Infinite and eternal love. This is what we were, and we knew it. We lived happily as one mind, and this is the way that it has always been. Then, for reasons of curiosity, we had a thought. It was a thought that was unnatural, and it denied everything that was true. One simple thought of deprivation and separation from ourselves. That's all that it took. It was one simple thought that created the Big Bang, and then the same silly thought encapsulated all the proceeding little bangs.

It was our false unnatural thought that instantly created the world that we know. Now because it only took an instant to project this world, we thought that it was always here. From that instant of the Big Bang and through all the proceeding little bangs and up until now, all of our unnatural thoughts were blamed on what we perceived. They were not seen as the cause of our own unseen projection. This is why the dream continued for thousands of years, because of the simultaneous nature of cause and effect, of projection and perception. The cause of the dream almost seems to hide itself and reverse the true nature of its origin. It may seem that whatever has happened was the cause of our unnatural thoughts, but it is the other way around.

It is the fear, guilt, and sin that people carry with them and repeat within their mind that is responsible for the continuation of the dream. In our perception we condemn what has happened, feel guilty about it, and then fear what is yet to occur. These particular thoughts are the basis of time, and they create the illusion of past, present, and, future. Do you understand?"

"Maybe," I said. "I'm not really sure."

"Well," she said. "Ask me something about it."

I sat back in my seat, unsure of what to ask. It seemed to me that she knew what she was talking about, but I wondered how she was so sure of what she was saying. She wasn't part of any religion or any kind of cult. So perhaps her motive was sincere and she truly wanted me to understand life. It seemed too good to be true.

"Okay," I said. "So what makes you so sure of what you say? That this is just a dream, I mean. Could it not be real? Because it feels real to me."

She laughed, and said, "Alright Mike, let's use that scientific mind of yours. Logically, all physical matter should be put into one category. Whether it is dream matter, or what people call real life matter. It should all be in one category of being either real or unreal. It cannot be both, am I right?"

"Yeah," I said. "I suppose, but why can't it all be real? Why does it have to be a dream?"

"Well," she said, as she poured a new glass of wine. "Is a dream that is structured any more real than a dream that is not? I mean, we already know for sure that dreams in the night are unreal. So logically it makes sense to put all physical experiences into this same category of unreality. What you consider to be your real life is a dream that you will wake from. It does not matter how real it looks and feels. It is a cycle of dreams, and you will wake from them."

"Okay," I said. "So you're talking about a cycle of dreams and thousands of years of evolving our thoughts. Does this mean that you believe in reincarnation?"

"Well," she said. "I do, but it's not real either." I took another long drink and finished off another beer.

"That doesn't make any sense," I said. "How can you say that you believe in it, and then say that it is not real?"

"Well," she said, "Just because you have had hundreds if not thousands of dreams does not change the fact that they were dreams. You've had hundreds if not thousands of identities, and only one of them is who you truly are. It is only helpful to believe in reincarnation so that you understand that your birth was not the beginning and your death will not be the end. Your life is eternal."

"So you pretty much just pick out parts from each religion that you agree with, and then just disregard the rest," I said.

"Something along those lines," she said. "Religion is a topic of which I have little interest, for it is yet another structured hierarchy of illusions. I mean, the idea that God must be reached indirectly is absurd. Do you really think that He would only make contact with only certain people and leave the rest of us in the dark?"

"No," I said. "I think that man took advantage of the word God as much as possible. Man has fulfilled his own personal desires by making people afraid of God, instead of loving God."

"That's right," she said. "But religions are not a bad thing. There are some incredible stories of people reaching God directly that would have been lost in the winds of time, had religions not passed them along. Which reminds me, who comes to mind for reaching God directly?"

"Jesus," I said. "Christianity is pretty big, and he is the main man in that religion."

"Yes," she said, "and what did he talk about? What was he most famous for preaching about and practicing?"

"Umm, forgiveness," I said.

"Bingo!" she said. "I want to talk to you a little bit about forgiveness and why we should do it. First I have to go pee, though, so watch my wine doesn't spill." She set her glass down on the bench beside me and started down the ladder. I was becoming very intrigued with our conversation, perhaps it was because I was starting to feel a little buzzed. I had four beers gone already and I knew that I would have to go pee soon as well.

"Ahh, fuck it", I thought to myself. I'm a guy, so that means that I can piss wherever I want. I stood up and walked to the edge of the tower. I leaned up against the corner wooden post facing the trees. I just opened my fly and let it flow, but suddenly I heard a screech from down below. I looked down to see Lucy looking up at me, and that I was urinating on her. She ran towards the cabin and I yelled out to her as she dashed.

"Oh my God!" I yelled, "I'm so sorry." Then I heard the cabin door slam, and I was all alone.

I finished up and sat back down. I felt like such an idiot. I couldn't believe that I had done that. It was the most embarrassing thing that had ever happened to me. For the next fifteen minutes I sat there condemning myself and worrying about what would come next. I didn't want to face Lucy when she came back. I was thinking of going home, as I had already caused enough damage.

Chapter 7

Just then the cabin door opened and Lucy walked out. She came right over to the tower and climbed up the ladder. I could hear her getting closer, and I spoke as soon as I could see the top of her head.

"I'm so sorry," I said again. "I feel terrible."

"Don't," she said immediately.

"What do you mean?" I said, "I peed on you. That is such a disgusting thing to do, and I don't deserve to be here anymore. I should just leave you alone, and not cause you any more hardship."

"Nonsense!" she said. "I like you here, and you can stay as long as you want." She was smiling, and sipping on her wine. It made me relax, but I couldn't believe that she wasn't upset.

"Yeah, but I peed on you!" I said as dramatically as I could, and she just laughed.

"Don't worry about it," she said. "I was just about to talk to you about forgiveness, but apparently I'll have to demonstrate it as well."

"I'm so sorry," I said once again. "I didn't mean to do that."

"You didn't do anything," she said, "and that never really

happened." Then she took out another joint and put it in her mouth. She lit it up, and took a long drag. A dark grey cloud came from her mouth as she exhaled, and it gently sat upon the crisp night air. She then took another puff and blew out another cloud of smoke.

"Forgive and forget what never was," she said, "and you will find what you are looking for." Then there was a silence, and I pondered what this meant. We sat in silence while she smoked her joint, and up until her last drag.

"Let's use the example of a dream once again," she said, as she butted it out. "Not the same one as before though, because you still remember it. Actually, tell me what that dream was about first, because there is probably a reason that you remember it."

"Oh it was just some silly dream that I had as a kid," I said.

"Okay," she said, "so tell me about it."

"Alright," I said. "I remember coming home from school one day on the bus and all of my possessions were laid out on the front lawn. Everything that I owned was all over the place, not where it should be. It was just kid's stuff, colouring books, toys, and whatnot. Anyway, I can vaguely remember running around trying to pick them all up. That's about all that I can remember."

She looked over at me. "Rather symbolic, don't you think?" she said calmly, as she slouched down on the bench.

"How do you mean?" I asked.

"Well," she said. "You were running around trying to pick up everything that you valued, but you probably have none of that stuff anymore."

"You're right," I said. "All that I have left from that time of my life is myself."

"Now you're getting it," she said. "While the world keeps changing, you remain a constant. No matter what happens, you will still be there afterwards. Even through death, you remain a constant as your body dissipates into nothing. You are still there, and you have free will.

Anyway, I want to get back to forgiveness, and what it means. Let's say that you have a dream, where something crazy is happening. During which you were completely terrified. Anyway, you wake up, and for a moment you aren't sure if the dream really happened, or if it was just a nightmare. Then, in the exact same instant two things happen simultaneously. You recognize that it was only a dream, and you forgive it.

This is the same with waking from the world we know into heaven. However, we do not wake from one dream and into another. We wake from all dreams and all experiences. The same instant that you recognize this world's unreality is the same instant that you will forgive it, and there are no exceptions to this.

There is a major difference between waking from a nightmare and waking from all dreams. When you wake from a nightmare, there are things in your 'real life' that are yet to be forgiven. However, when you wake from all dreams, you forgive everything and everyone. The feeling of this is indescribable."

"Umm," I muttered, and interrupted her. "Do you forgive everyone and everything? Just like when I peed on you, which, don't forget was an accident." She laughed.

"Yeah that was a pretty fucked up dream, wasn't it?" she said. "That's all that it was, though Mike, a fucked up dream. So you can forgive yourself, and forget about it. Forgive and forget what never was, and you will find what you are looking for."

As she spoke those words for the second time I melted in my seat. It felt so good to feel true forgiveness, and those words made sense to me now. I thought about how badly I had tortured myself following the incident, and it all meant nothing now. I felt a sense of euphoria.

"Peace is the natural outcome of forgiveness, Mike," she said, and she was telling me exactly what I was feeling. "Take the nightmare again, for example. If you wake up and still believe that it really happened, then you will be terrified until you recognize that it hadn't happened. Then all of the terrifying thoughts disappear, and you forget about it.

I cannot describe how wonderful it feels to wake up from all experiences, but this is what I am helping you to do. Forgiveness is the key to the gates of heaven, but I am not telling you to forgive. What I am telling you about is the unreality of the world that you see, so that forgiveness will be inevitable. Because if you can truly recognize a dream as just that, a dream, then there is no way that you cannot truly forgive it. Once the world is completely forgiven, then that beholder no longer witnesses it. They become aware of reality, and dreams are forgotten forever."

"So is this what you think Jesus did?" I asked. "He recognized that this world was just a dream, so he couldn't help but to forgive us. Is that why you think that he returned to heaven?"

"Yeah, I think so," she said. "I don't think that Christianity would support such an idea, but how else could one completely forgive the world? I mean, just put yourself in his shoes for a minute. If someone tortures you and nails you to a cross, you're not going to forgive them if you believe that it is really happening. There is no way to truly forgive the guilty, but it is incredibly easy to forgive the innocent.

So to me, it looks as if Jesus forgave us for our sins because he recognized that we were innocent. But how could we be truly innocent if we really crucified him? Therefore he must have recognized the unreality of this world and that none of this is really happening. He must have realized what the rest of us are just finding out now."

"Yeah," I said. "I suppose you could be right. I grew up in a Christian family, but I never really understood the glorification of Jesus. I mean, he was our brother. He was a person just like us, but they made it seem like he was better than us. They said that he was the only son of God, but where does that leave us? I couldn't understand the theology behind it.

This is the reason that I lost faith in God, and everything religious. I mean, I didn't have much doubt that Jesus knew what he was doing at the time, but I didn't trust the church leaders to interpret it for me. Such as when Jesus said that he forgave us for all of our sins. They seemed to interpret this as meaning that Jesus already did all of the forgiving, so we don't have to forgive ourselves."

"I see," she said. "Yeah, he forgave us in his own mind, and that is why he was released. He set an example for us, but we must completely forgive as he did."

"And you say that recognizing the unreality of this world brings with it true forgiveness." I said.

"That's right," she said. "For why would you condemn someone for something that never happened? Why would you hold guilt over something that isn't real? Why would you fear that which could never occur?"

"True," I said, "but I still can't believe that this world isn't real. It has so much structure to it, and order."

"Is a dream that is structured any more real than a dream that is not?" she said, reminding me once again of the similarity of all experiences.

"So are you waking from all dreams?" I asked. "How can you be so sure of yourself?"

"It was two weeks after I moved out here," she said. "With all the hustle and bustle of town I didn't have much time to think, but out here was different. I could relax and put my feet up. I was no longer at the whim of someone else's fingertips and on call at all hours. I finally had time to myself. Anyway, so two weeks after moving out here I was pondering what that patient had told me so long ago, and I had a moment of clarity.

I was lying in bed in the dark, and for a moment I completely forgave the world. It was a wonderful feeling, and along with this feeling there was something else as well. A pure white light came across my vision, and completely surrounded me. There was no artificial or natural light present, but there I was, immersed in light. I was joined with it! A light so pure that it must have been of God, for it was beyond anything I have ever seen in this world. Pure and undivided, as were my thoughts at the time.

You might think that I was just stoned, but if I had only seen the light then I would have demanded a scientific explanation. It was not so much the light that captivated me, but the feeling, and the awareness of being awake from all experiences. I cannot describe it in words. It was heaven, and nothing short of this."

"So are you saying that you were in heaven?" I asked, a little bit sarcastically.

"Yeah," she said. "If this had never happened, then there is no way that I would be telling you this stuff right now. I would still be an atheist and unsure of what is real. However, now I am certain that heaven is real and this world is a dream."

"I see," I said, "that's pretty cool. So what's heaven like?" I think she could detect my sarcasm, but it didn't seem to bother her.

"If I could describe to you what heaven is like," she said, "then I would. It is indescribable, however, and all that I have are words to describe. Love is the highest word that I can think of, and even this means nothing in and of itself.

Therefore, I am better off to describe the unreality of the world that is fear, and show you how foolish it really is. This is my job, as was given to me by God in heaven. And so I must fulfill it and be rewarded with my simple awareness of His eternal love."

"Wow," I said. "That's pretty deep. It must be an important job if God is your boss." I laughed, polishing off my fifth beer.

"I wouldn't say that he is my boss," she said. "Remember that I said we are God, but not who we might think we are. When you look at the world through forgiving eyes, then the fear and hate seem totally ridiculous. Seeing your brothers at war while you are at peace makes you want to help them. What they do to themselves is foolish, and you want them to see the light. It only becomes natural to let them know that they but dream a dream, and that there is nothing to fear."

"So you fancy yourself a teacher then, eh?" I asked, almost consciously trying to bring her down to my level.

"One must be a teacher in order to learn," she said. "Everyone teaches, and learns from what they teach, for example, when you taught me about your theory about Mars and the moon and all that stuff. Did you not learn something from teaching me that?"

"I suppose I did," I said.

"Well," she said. "What did you learn?"

I looked up at the stars and tried to examine what I had learned. The night sky was brilliant, and there was no light pollution to dilute its intricate design.

"I suppose I learned that even if my theory was true, it is still rather meaningless, and it would not answer any real questions," I said. "But rather, it opens up more meaningless questions, leaving us with the questions that we have always struggled with.

The questions of who we are, what we are doing here, and why? These are probably most important, and to be honest Lucy, I hope to God that you are right. I hope that this is only a dream, and that we have nothing to worry about." I was feeling pretty drunk now, but this was allowing me to express myself sincerely. I actually did hope that she was right, and that I was wrong.

"Look up," I said. "Just look at that cluster of stars. If our little blue planet is in the hands of that fucking thing, then surely we are all doomed. An explosion of that magnitude will surely be the end of us all. Think of the black holes for instance, so powerful that not even the ether can escape its draw. Leaving no medium to transfer light, we are left to judge their presence by watching suns like ours get sucked into them. It is such a crazy universe out there!" I was starting to get upset now, just thinking of all the hazards that we face. "Our sun was hurtled out of that raging fire like a spark, and it will inevitably be enveloped by the same fire."

"Calm down Mike," she said. "The salvation of the world involves recognizing the complete lack of danger that it faces, and nothing else. We are not in the hands of that spiral of uncontrollable energy. We are in the hands of God, and it is impossible that he drop us. What is real can never die, look at me Mike." I looked at her, and my face lost all expression. Her eyes were deep, and she looked like she really cared.

"You cannot die," she said. "What is real can never die, and you are more real than anything that you can see. The world will falter and fade, while you remain strong and pure. You are a perfect eternal being, and I want you to be aware of this. What is true can never die, and what is false shall fade before your eyes." I immediately felt better, and couldn't help but to accept what she was telling me.

I was never one to refuse praises, and what she was telling me was more than I could ever hope for. What more could I ever want than to be eternally perfect? What more could anyone want? She was describing the pureness of our being, and how our experiences do not alter it. She had only talked to me a few times, and already she had torn apart everything that I believed in. Only she didn't leave me with nothing, instead she offered pure love and respect. It was something that could not be described with simple words, but only with a feeling.

"How can I thank you?" I asked, breaking a silence that had lasted several minutes. "How can I thank you for everything that you've done for me?" She chuckled, and sipped her wine with a devious looking smirk on her face.

"What?" I asked, and she laughed again, almost choking on her wine, and she had to sit up straight. "What is it?" I asked again.

"Nothing," she said. "You don't want to know."

"Oh, come on!" I said. "Now you have to tell me."

"Alright," she said. "You go down and stand under the tower, because I really have to pee, and I still have to get you back."

"Oh, go on!" I said, almost yelling.

"I seriously do have to go pee again though," she said. "So watch this shit for me." She set down her wine, and another joint that she must have brought up before. "Do you need anything while I'm down Mike?" she asked just before disappearing down the ladder.

"No, I'm good, but thanks," I said, as I leaned back on the bench. "Yes ma'am", I thought, "I am good". I picked up the joint that she had left and rolled it through my fingers. It looked and felt as if it had been made in a factory. It had the perfect texture and the perfect shape. I was sure that she had rolled a lot of them before this, and as they say, practice makes perfect. I wondered if I should partake in the smoking of this joint, as I had not tried it since my high school days.

She came back up without me noticing, until she spoke, almost scaring the shit out of me.

"Are you going to help me smoke that, or what?" she asked, and I broke a smile just thinking about it.

"Possibly," I said. "I haven't had any since high school, and I forget what it's like."

"Well," she said, as she sat back down beside me. "You can try it if you want, but you certainly don't have to."

"What the hell!" I said. "I'll give it a whirl, but I'm fairly drunk, so I might not feel it as much." She lit it up, and handed me the joint. I took a long drag and inhaled the smoke, holding it in my lungs. I blew out a huge cloud of smoke and started coughing. I coughed so hard that my stomach felt sick and I couldn't handle it anymore. I handed it back to her, as I tried to recover.

"That's good for me," I said. "That stuff is harsh!"

Peter G. MacFarlane

After a moment my coughing finally stopped, and I watched her as she smoked the rest of that rancid stuff.

"How can you smoke that stuff?" I asked. "There is an obvious reason that it's illegal. Fucking damn near killed me!"

"Nobody has ever died from smoking weed," Lucy said, laughing. "But think about how many people die from alcohol poisoning and drunken car crashes. It's funny how they make weed illegal, while a very deadly drug like alcohol is legal."

"So you don't think that weed should be illegal, eh?" I said.

"I don't think that anything should be illegal," she said. "People are going to do whatever they want to anyway, so placing limits on them is fairly pointless. In fact, it encourages people to rebel and go against the grains of society. I don't think that there should be laws, rules, or commandments of any kind. People are decent enough that they are not going to kill one another if all of a sudden murder is legalized. People are more civil than they used to be.

We are all beginning to realize that harming our brothers is the same as harming ourselves. So unless we want to feel hurt, then it makes sense to love one another. To put aside what makes us all appear to be different and find the common ground that binds us together. I believe that in the next few years there will be a total liberation of all burdens upon mankind. No more false barriers will dilute our free will, and the world will rise together as one. Coming together with one true will for happiness, and releasing the will to limit and control."

"Well," I said. "Why now? What do you think is really going on here?"

"Think of the evolving mind," she said. "Think about how all of our minds have been evolving together for thousands of years, and how only a few stray ones have found God before us. Like Jesus, Buddha, and others. Well, now the collective population has reached the point where finding God is easy.

The average person is changing the way that they look at the world, and consequently they become happier. It is a beautiful time to be on this Earth. The average person has reached the point of potential enlightenment and wisdom. The only thing that is stopping them is their loosening grip on the world that they used to know.

The days of war, hatred, and any form of conflict are over, as one person finds God so do a thousand, and a thousand more after that. A very small ripple of God's love and wisdom can grow into an enormous wave very quickly. As each early morning moment brings us a little more light, so does each passing day give us a little more sight. It is the unfolding of something beautiful, and the dawning of something majestic.

What more can I say, but this? What more could I ever do, but to give you my word, and assurance that love is real? That there is a truth beyond the words that I speak, and that I didn't make it all up."

"I believe you," I said. "I'm not really a hundred percent sure of what you are saying, but I have faith in you. You sound too sincere to be making it all up."

"Do you know what the hardest part of it all was?" she said, "about accepting that it is only a dream."

"What?" I asked.

"That I didn't figure it out all by myself." She said, "Someone else had told me that it was a dream, and I didn't figure it out all by myself. My name would never go down in history for listening to someone else, but do you know what?"

"What?" I said.

"It doesn't matter, because Lucy Crane is an illusory identity that does not need to be remembered. I mean, my name will not be Lucy Crane after I pass away, so why would I want people to remember that name? What I want people to remember is what I came to represent. I want them to remember our oneness, and unity in God."

"Wow," I said. "That's pretty deep!"

We sat there in the peace of our union, and I felt a deep

connection towards her. She seemed to exude unconditional love and forgiveness. She had let me know everything that I had ever needed to know, but I knew that it would be my job to accept it. That would be the hardest part, I thought. To accept that no matter what happened I would be safe in the comfort of God's loving hands.

"Thank you," I said quietly. She didn't respond, but I knew that she heard me. From thence on we didn't speak. There was no need to, because we could feel each others thoughts. It was not an awkward silence, but one of quiet reflection and jubilation, for peace had come.

An hour of this passed, and now the booze was running low. I only had three beers left, and I didn't feel like finishing them. Lucy was on her final glass of wine. "How are you feeling now?" I asked her.

"Pretty drunk, actually," she said. "Are you ready to call it a night?"

"Yeah," I said, as I took the last swig of my beer. I grabbed the remaining three, and we both stood up. I was tired, and I think that she was too.

I slept on the floor that night, but it wasn't very comfortable. I tossed and turned until the wee hours of the morning. Lucy had given me a pillow and blanket, but the hardness of the floor kept me awake. At the first sign of light the birds rang in the new day, and it wasn't until this that I fell asleep. Only it was a restless sleep, and I must have slipped into a dream.

Lucy and I were down by the river sitting on the bench and I was reliving what had happened earlier. I leaned back on the bench, and said, "Well I think that you could be right, but to me this world is very much real. I cannot conceive of the idea that this world is just a dream. This bench is real," I said, as I slapped it. I could feel the sharp, rough edges of the bench piercing my hand.

"Okay," she said. "Well, say you have a dream about this same conversation tonight. Will you still think that it is real when you wake up?" I stood up and walked towards the river. I picked up a rock and squeezed it. The rock was hard and it fit perfectly within my hand.

"I don't understand it," I yelled back to her. The next thing I knew, her hand was on my shoulder and she was looking me in the eyes.

"Don't worry, it will be alright," she said softly. She then took the rock from my hand and held it up. "This rock," she said, "It is an illusion. It is not really there, but you are."

"What?" I said, just as the dream ceased to be, and I sat up on the hard floor. It took me a few seconds to remember where I was, but as I did, I also remembered what I had dreamt about, and the irony sunk in. I had felt the same way in the dream as I had yesterday. I truly thought that it was real, and that I really had been down by the river. The implications of this dream were great, for what more proof did I need?

"What more affirmation do I need than this?" I thought. To be told that this world is not real, that it is no more than a dream. Then to have a dream about being told this, and truly believing it to be real. The implications of waking from this dream were outstanding, for it removed all faith that one has in the physical world. At that moment, everything that Lucy had told me made sense. It was a dream.

I looked over to see that Lucy was sound asleep with a huge grin on her face, as if she were totally happy and at peace with herself. I sat there with the blanket wrapped around me, as the cabin felt cool. Recollecting the memories of previous events, I wondered what to do next. Lucy was still fast asleep, but sleep was not an option for me anymore. I decided to get up and take a peek outside.

It was still early morning, as the sun was yet to warm the earth. Dew spread across the grass and glistened in the growing sunlight. "Too early for me", I thought, but I couldn't sleep on that floor anymore. I decided that I should go home and have a nice long sleep. It was warm and comforting just to think of lying in my own bed. So I grabbed the last three beers and took one more look around the cabin.

Lucy still had that same look on her face, and I thought that I'd best not be waking her. I watched her face as I closed the door to leave. She had such a peaceful look on her face, with not a single hint of discomfort. There was no way that she could be having a nightmare, or even dreams of any kind.

I walked back to the car and drove home, once again profoundly intrigued by the philosophy of this lady. It seemed to me that whatever she had found was the true answer, and she was revealing it all to me. "I wish that I could understand it more deeply", I thought, "and use it in my own life". Happiness is something that cannot be bought, but it is something that is given freely by those who know its true source.

However, it still seemed to me that this world was real, that it couldn't possibly be a dream. I could feel the steering wheel's soft texture in my hands and the wind flowing through my hair. It seemed about as real as it can get. On the other hand, the dream that I had should be my proof and remove my faith from that which is unreal. For no matter how hard the rock felt, and no matter how real the dream appeared to be, waking up just throws it all out the window and renders the whole thing unreal.

When I got home I had a very long sleep, and it was a pleasure for my aching muscles. It was one of the most beautiful sleeps that I've ever had. I was fairly happy when I went to sleep and even happier when I awoke. The sun shined in through the window blind and cast lines of light that streaked across the bed next to me. Normally I would find this annoying, but today it was a gentle reminder of a bright new day in progress. I had what could almost be considered a hangover, but not enough to ruin my morning.

Just as I was getting out of bed, I had a sudden urge to return to Lucy's, but I had no reason to go. With no explanation for this urge I would be a fool to go, I thought, but the urge was too great. So I gave in, and jumped in the car without hesitation. I figured that this trip could be justified in one way or another, and that in the end its reason would be sure. It was a decision that had to be made in faith, and not in doubt.

When I arrived at the cabin, the door was open and there was an old man leaning over the bed. I could not understand what was going on, and as I walked in the man turned around. "Oh my God", I thought, it was the old man from the liquor store. His face was old and rigid and surely it was the same man. I could not forget that face.

"Hello," he said. Tears rolled down his face, and his eyes seemed to hold a solid layer of tears ready to fall. I looked to the bed, and Lucy was lying there. Her face appearing the exact same as when I had left.

"What happened?" I asked.

"She's dead," he said, his voice cracking as he spoke. "Lucy called me this morning. I'm her father, Oscar Crane. Anyway, she called me late this morning. All that she told me was that she was waking up now, and that she couldn't sleep anymore. I asked her what she meant by that, and she said something else, and then hung up." He stopped talking, and stared at the wall, as if he were no longer sad.

"What did she say?" I asked him.

He looked at me and said, "What she told me, I don't think I can do. I'm too old, and my time is limited. Perhaps you are supposed to do it."

"What did she say?" I asked again, anxiously waiting to hear what she had said, while still in a state of shock.

"She said: 'Tell the world that I love them all very much'." He looked back at Lucy, and leaned over, kissing her on the forehead. I stood there, unsure of what to make of the situation. It was all too much, and I couldn't understand how it could have happened.

"Well," I said. "Did you call an ambulance, or what happened?"

"Yes," he said. "They are on their way. I called them when I got here and found that she wasn't breathing and had no pulse. I have no idea what happened, but she is definitely dead.

For the past two years she's been telling me that death isn't real and that we are not really bodies. I don't know where she found the faith to believe such things, but she was awfully sure of herself. She would tell this to whoever would listen, and it didn't really matter who it was. Who are you by the way?" he asked. I was still in shock, and unclear about the situation.

"Umm, I'm Mike Love," I said. "Lucy saved me from a car crash, and I came to visit a couple of times." He just nodded his head and looked away.

Suddenly a disgusting reality dawned on me. I was here last night, and now Lucy is dead. Of course I knew that I had nothing to do with it, but a misjudgement could be made very easily in this case. Here was an unexplained death with me being the last person to see her alive. "But wait!" I thought. No one knew that I was here last night, and for all anyone knew, I was at home. It was the perfect alibi to a crime that I didn't commit. If anyone asked me, then that is where I was, and nobody was the wiser. Should it come up, of course, but I figured I'd better limit what I said.

Just then, two paramedics walked through the door and took over the situation. They checked her vital signs and assessed the possibility of resuscitation. It was hopeless, as was expected by everyone present. So Oscar and I watched as the two men loaded Lucy onto a stretcher and covered her with a sheet. It was a sombre moment indeed, yet with a hint of hope.

What Lucy gave to the world could best be described as a remembrance of peace, I thought. She gave a silent salute to a feeling and a reality that we had almost forgotten. Her life was a joyful praise to love and the common ground that binds us all together. Of course, her name will be swept away by the winds of time, but what she spoke of is as eternal as she. Truly, she was a wise woman.

As they took her away, I stayed by the cabin door until they were out of sight. Oscar had gone with them, and I was left there by myself. I gathered up the empty liquor bottles from the night before, which were the only evidence that I had ever been there. I was about to leave for the last time when I noticed something on the nightstand beside her bed.

On a little piece of paper were the words written, 'Forgive and forget what never was, and you will find what you are looking for. I will be with you all of the way, and I have perfect faith that you will succeed. Failure is impossible, for your will coincides with that of the will of God.' I put the piece of paper in my pocket, and left that place. Never to return again, but the memories always remained fresh in my mind.

I never forgot about my experiences there, but unfortunately I never spoke of them again either. I retained an unjustified fear that I would be blamed for the death of Lucy Crane, and this is what kept me from telling her story. Such as the beautiful conversations that we had and the unconditional love that she gave. None of this would ever pass through my lips, nor be scripted through my hand. It was to remain forever unwritten, and untold.

Chapter 8

I spent the next two days on the couch at home. Depression had come to me, and it had suffocated any remaining faith that I had in a higher power. Lucy had been the only one who had ever sincerely wanted to help me overcome fear, and now she was gone. Even she, who had spoken of eternal life, faced death, and now her presence was as phony as God's.

I felt as if love were something of which I was unworthy, and that I was to remain forever bound to the physical. As my body disintegrated, then so should I, and I would become the complete absence of anything. This was my destiny, but my will was for something else. My will was that neither I nor anyone else should die. "It is too bad that free will is a lie", I thought, "and that my will shall always be confined to the physical limitations of my decaying body."

I recall sitting there in front of the tube, and feeling like the dirt between the toes of society. I felt about as low as one can get, and then for no reason, I reached for my wallet. I still had the piece of paper that I took from Lucy's cabin, and I pulled it out. Reading those words again caused shivers to run through my spine, and I felt the presence of someone else in the room. I could only assume that it was Lucy, but I had no idea. I was never one to believe in ghosts, but at the same time I could not deny the feeling that I was not alone.

Somehow I was able to draw energy from this presence, and I stood up, holding the piece of paper. I read the words aloud, "Forgive and forget what never was, and you will find what you are looking for. I will be with you all of the way, and I have perfect faith that you will succeed. Failure is impossible, for your will coincides with that of the will of God." I felt like a soldier standing at attention, but my training was in preparation for peace. I stood there in a moment of silence with a renewed affirmation that everything that Lucy had told me was right.

I sat back down, and felt a million times better. It was beautiful. Just then the phone rang, and I calmly walked over to retrieve it.

"Hello," I said.

"Hello," a raspy voice answered. "Is this Mike Love?" His voice was so decrepit that it sounded as though he said, 'Is this my love?' I almost burst out laughing into the phone, but held it in.

"Yes," I replied. "Who is this?"

"This is Oscar Crane. Do you remember me? I am Lucy's father."

"Oh yes," I said. "How are you doing?"

"Good," he said. "I just called to see if you were getting along alright. I didn't see you at the wake today, and I was wondering if you plan to attend the funeral." I hesitated, and couldn't think of what I should say. I hadn't planned on going, since I had only just met her before she died.

"I'm not sure," I said. "I have no idea where it is at."

"Do you know where the hospital is?" he asked.

"Yes," I said.

"Well," he said. "The funeral is going to be held in the church directly across the street from the hospital. You can't miss it. It is going to be at eleven o'clock in the morning, and we would really appreciate it if you would come. I know that Lucy affected a lot of people in very deep and mystical way, and we want to share our stories with one another. There are even some writings that she had left behind, and we are going to read them aloud."

"Okay," I said. "I will be there."

"Great," he said. "Have a nice night Mike."

"You too," I replied, and then I hung up the phone. I walked back to the couch, and didn't know what to think of that. I had been feeling like shit about ten minutes ago, and now I didn't. It was strange that Oscar had phoned me just as I was being lifted from my depression. Now I had something to attend tomorrow, and even though it was a funeral, I felt that it would be positive. So, I shaved, showered, and went to bed earlier than usual.

The next morning I arose before the sun, but not because I wanted to. I couldn't sleep, and it was because I was thinking of Lucy. She had dismantled my entire belief in science by using dreams as examples, and from what I could tell it was all true.

The physical matter that one observes within a dream seems very real, but only while one is dreaming of it. So perhaps the world that we see is only a dream, and we are wasting our time thinking that it is real. There is an even deeper meaning to all of this, I thought, and our happiness depends upon it.

If each one of us can reach the point at which all experiences are truly recognized as unreal, or as simple dreams, than total forgiveness is inevitable, and we will become as happy as is possible. If all is forgiven, then we will wake up from all experiences and this is what is known as heaven. No conflicting thoughts, nor any conflicting dreams to their effect. In heaven there is infinite eternal love, and nothing short of this.

"I can't even begin to imagine what it would be like", I thought, "and I'm not going to try just yet". The sun was showing the first signs that there would be a new day to come, and I fell back down on the bed. I let out a long yawn, and figured that I should try to sleep again before the sun completely rose. I fell asleep with a big smile on my face. Just feeling happy to be here and alive, and then five hours passed me by within an instant.

It was now ten o'clock, and I started to panic when I realized the time. I only had an hour before the funeral, and the drive alone would take me twenty minutes. I scrambled to make a crude breakfast as I attentively watched the clock on the wall. Burnt toast and partially cooked eggs had to do the trick, and I raced to get dressed.

I threw on my trusty old tuxedo that had gotten me through several formal occasions and then I proceeded to put on my tie with much frustration. It took me a while, but finally I was able to get the tie to look just right. It was rather a difficult procedure with only one working hand, but somehow I had managed. I dashed out the door and was on the road in a matter of seconds. I quickly turned on the radio and made myself as comfortable as possible. It was a nice day and there was not a cloud in the sky.

I began to think about Lucy again, and what she was trying to tell me. The impending funeral would bring much insight, I thought, and perhaps it would reveal to me her true message. Oscar had asked me to tell the world that Lucy loved them all very much, but how was I to give such a message? I did not understand her true message as of yet, and I still had this fear of being blamed for her death.

"I can't tell anyone that I was there the night before", I thought, "Because that would be too suspicious". Perhaps my best course of action would be to stay completely within the shadows, observing what the others had to say. As far as I knew there was still no explanation for her death, and I couldn't risk the incorrect judgement that I was guilty of murder. Hopefully there would be some mention of an autopsy, or something would come up that would relieve my fear.

I saw myself as being full of horrid thoughts as I drove towards a rotten destiny. "How long before I can see the light?" I thought to myself, as I looked to the sun. "I truly want to have peace, but yet I am holding onto everything that prevents it. I have built a wall around love, and for some reason I refuse to tear it down". It was strange, and at the same time it was enlightening. I put myself at the cause of what I was feeling, and not at the effect of what was happening. I could not blame the world for anything.

Something changed in me just then, and I threw my fears out the window. Emancipated and free of external judgement, I was the judge of myself. What would I proclaim myself as, other than completely innocent? It occurred to me that it didn't really matter what other people thought of me, but rather my own judgement was of top priority. Once again my mood was becoming lightened, as if Lucy had just explained it to me all over again.

For the rest of the trip my mind was healed and at peace. The simple idea that Lucy had introduced to me was almost unbelievable. I was now in control, and I could choose not to project anything that I would rather not perceive. The world that surrounded me was a reflection of my own thoughts, and at the moment those reflections were beautiful. My soul was shining within my open mind, as was the sun shining within the open sky.

I seemed to transcend time while I was in this state, and before I knew it I was at the church. I pulled into the parking lot and parked in one of the few remaining spots near the road. There were other people who were just arriving, and I was thankful that I was not late. There were quite a lot of cars, and I couldn't believe that this many people knew Lucy.

I got out of the car and slowly walked towards the church. It was such a beautiful day, but it had such a mournful purpose. The thought of death seemed to weigh down on people's shoulders, as nobody appeared to be holding their head high.

I was one of them, and my eyes met only the floor as I walked into the church. I quickly found a seat at the back next to an old man I did not recognize.

It had been over a decade since the last time that I was in a church, and my gaze almost automatically turned to the ceiling. The architectural design of this particular building was incredible, and the shear height of the dome-shaped ceiling above was remarkable. It was like walking into a time capsule, and witnessing the detailed craftsmanship of a generation gone past. It was something that people could no longer withstand to produce in this modern age and still have enough money to run the show.

There were large pillars standing to support the structure, and one of them was right in front of me. It was large enough to partially block my view of the altar, but that was no big deal. The cover that it provided from leering eyes was more than enough to justify my chosen seat. Besides, I thought, I came here with the intentions of staying in the shadows and not being seen. A large pillar of obscurity was just what I needed.

I looked around the room, but saw only unfamiliar faces. I recognized no one, and everyone else seemed to be looking around as well. Loud whispers could be heard throughout the church, as well as the shuffling feet of a few final stragglers. Then the room fell quiet, and the anticipation rose dramatically. A young man steadily walked up the aisle, approaching the podium with confidence. I could no longer see him, but his voice was clear as he began to speak.

"Hello everyone," he said. "My name is Richard Donaldson, and I have been close friends with Lucy for a very long time. I like to think that I knew her as well as anyone else did, but she knew me even better than I know myself. Somehow she was able to see through my body and directly into my soul. She was somehow able to put aside all of our differences, and revel in the beauty of our similarities.

I know that Lucy affected a lot of different people, and I

can see that as I look around this room. It doesn't really matter who you are, or where you come from. We are all here for the same reason, and that is because Lucy no longer appears to us in form. We must find the faith that she is here with us in spirit, or else we will be forever grieving the terrible loss of a loving friend.

As most of you probably know, Lucy had an unusual way of looking at the world, and she was not afraid to tell people about it. She didn't see the world as most of us do, and her way of looking at it was very profound. She could see unity, but not division. She could see positive, but not negative. She could see love, but not hate. So in the name of love I request that our gathering here be seen as a celebration of eternal life, and not a proclamation of death."

The room was silent again, and the young man left the podium. Then the voice of a woman filled the room, but I could not see her. She was either obscured by the pillar in front of me or on the balcony above me. Other people who could see the alter were gawking around as well, so I could only assume that she was on the balcony.

"This is a song that Lucy wrote", she said, but if you have ever heard Lucy sing, then you'll know why I am going to sing it for her."

An acoustic guitar began to play, and it resonated throughout the building. As the song began, I paid close attention to the lyrics, and was struck by the message within. It was a song about love and the senselessness of hate. It was just a simple poem, but it was intertwined within a beautiful song. I recall seeing the faces of those who were struck by the powerful message that was delivered, and they looked as if they were witnessing heaven itself.

A long applause followed the song, and the young man returned to the podium. Already I had forgotten his name, but it didn't matter. The overall sensation in the room was now one of love, and a simple name was of little importance. The message that he was delivering far exceeded what could be accredited to one individual, but only to the wisdom of God. All differences were now set aside, and everyone shared the identity of love.

"The dream that divides the dreamers," he said, "does not exist, and nor does the time that seems to separate now and forever. This means that time and space do not exist, but we do. I am here now, and we are everywhere forever. We are one mind, but given free will, we have attempted division. This is all that we have ever done in this world. Set our minds to accomplish the impossible, and attempt to divide what must remain as one. It takes much resistance to maintain these dreams of division, and it is entirely unnecessary. With free will we can choose to allow oneness in our vision and see through the thin dream of distance. It is our destiny."

I'm sorry, but I was taken in by those words. I can no longer continue witnessing my failures in such detail, and I must continue my soul experience of life. So I think that I will carry on now and accelerate the rest of my life review. All that is required is the will to do so. I will not carefully examine the last months of my life. They were spent worrying about being blamed and fearing my impending death. I have better things to do than dwell on my own faults and mistakes. I can make things right again!

BAM! An instant passed, and so did the rest of my life review. It was like a knife in the heart, but it was my thoughts that hurt the most. Fear, sin, and guilt reigned over my mind and disallowed any pure thoughts of love. What Lucy had taught me about this world being a dream was obscured by a blanket of fear. Leaving no room to express what she had told me, and leaving Sharon in the dark to these revolutionary ideas.

Now I am sure that with my passing Sharon's life will be mournful, and she may even attempt her own demise. She will believe that death is real, and that we are torn apart forever. Never will she understand our eternal nature, until she surpasses death herself. Only then will she see that I am still alive, but that is not when it is needed.

We will never have truly expressed our eternal union, while the world seemed to separate us. We will never have had that be all and end all conversation. The type of conversing that ties up any loose ends through forgiveness, and clarity of vision. It must be performed in the world of division, as to put an end to it forever.

These thoughts loom in my mind, as my life review is now complete and I sit upon a void. I wish that I could go back and tell the story of Lucy Crane. I wish that I could go back and tell everyone everything. In one form or another, I would express to the world what is true and what is eternal. But most of all, I wish that I could go back and tell Sharon that death isn't real. So that she will not fear it, as I did.

Wait! I see a light, in the distance. It is a different kind of light, one that the world never sees. I am moving towards it now, and it seems to be growing around me. Suddenly I am completely surrounded by this light, and I feel at home. I have a complete awareness of my true reality, and there is a feeling here that can only be described as pure sweet love. It is everyone in the entire world united as one, and there is no hatred here. There is no dream to divide the dreamers. It is heaven. I am safe here, and I know this.

Yes! I know this place. This is where I always am, but I forget about it when I'm dreaming. This is where I was after I crashed my truck and then I decided to go back into my dream. This is free will! It was my will to return to the dream when I had crashed, and that's exactly what I did. This means that I can go back at any time and tell everyone about Lucy.

With that one single thought, I was hurtled back into the dream within an instant. The laws of time and space mattered not, because I was creating them. I will to relive it once again, I thought, and do things differently this time. This is my will, and my will be done! My eyelids popped open with a crack, and I could feel the cool air rushing in to greet my waking eyes. I give thanks to God, for I now have a hand to write, and a mouth to speak.